The Happy Hollisters and the Mystery in Skyscraper City

By Jerry West

Illustrated by Helen S. Hamilton

GARDEN CITY, N.Y.

Doubleday & Company, Inc.

Library of Congress Catalog Card Number 59-7921

Contents

CHAPTER 1

A *MYSTERIOUS MESSAGE*

"*Secret Tunnels of New York City,*" Pete Hollister read aloud to his sister Pam. "Crickets! This ought to be an exciting book."

The blond, twelve-year-old boy picked up the volume from the table at the annual book sale in Lincoln School library. The place was crowded with children on the last day of school before summer vacation.

"What do you think of this, Pam?" Pete asked.

Pam, who was ten and had fluffy golden hair, glanced at the first page. "It sounds spooky and mysterious," she said, smiling. "And only twenty-five cents. Let's buy it."

"Okay." Pete made his way to the desk of Miss Allen, the librarian, and gave her a quarter for the purchase.

"I hope you enjoy reading about those secret tunnels, Pete," the sweet-faced, gray-haired woman said.

"I'm sure I will, Miss Allen. I like mysteries."

Pete's blue eyes sparkled as he thumbed through his new book. Suddenly two pages near the back opened wide. Between them was a folded piece of paper. Curious, Pete opened it, and saw that the sheet was covered with black, spidery-looking Oriental symbols.

"Oh, Pam," Pete called out, "look at this!" The girl hurried to his side, and both eagerly examined the strange writing.

"There's one word in English," Pam said excitedly, pointing to the bottom of the paper. "It says, 'Help.' "

"That's odd," Pete remarked. "I wonder what the other writing means?" He looked in the front of the book for the owner's name, but there was none.

Pam thought that perhaps a person in trouble had written the note and slipped it between the pages, hoping someone would find it.

"I wonder when the note was put in," Pete mused. "This book was published fifteen years ago," he added, looking at the date.

"But maybe the note has been in only a short time," Pam suggested. "Perhaps we are the first ones to find it." Pam was a kind-hearted girl and always wanted to help others who were in trouble. "Let's take the note home and show Mother," she said.

Pete opened the book again. "If we could find out who gave this to the sale, maybe the mystery would be solved."

He asked the librarian, but she could not help the children. "I never list the people who bring in the books, so I have no idea who gave this one."

Just then a boy named Joey Brill leaned over Pete's shoulder to see what was going on. He was larger than Pete, although the same age. Joey had played mean tricks on the Hollisters ever since the family had moved to Shoreham.

"What's that writing?" Joey asked as Pam studied the note.

"It's only a message in a foreign language," Pete said. "Maybe Japanese or Chinese."

"Let me take a look at it," Joey demanded.

Even before Pam could hand the piece of paper to him, Joey snatched it out of her hand.

"Don't do that!" Pete said, angered at the boy's rudeness.

Joey held the note high over his head and grinned. "It isn't really yours, anyhow," he taunted.

"The note was in this book Pete bought," Pam protested. "Give it back, Joey."

Joey lowered the paper and glanced at it quickly. "This is Egyptian writing," he said importantly, "and doesn't mean a thing. You won't need it any more."

"Hand that note over!" Pete said hotly.

By this time other children in the library had heard the conversation and turned their attention to the bully.

"What if I don't?" Joey sneered.

"Then I'll take it!" Pete retorted, leaning toward the taller boy.

"Try it!"

Pete reached for the note, but Joey again held it high over his head. Then as Pete pulled the bully's arm down, Joey pushed him in the face.

Pam cried out, "Stop that, you meanie!"

The librarian glanced up in time to see Pete twist Joey's arm until the note fluttered from his grip. Pam quickly reached over, picked up the paper and put it back into the book.

"Oh, you want to fight, eh?" Joey said, his face turning red with embarrassment.

Before Pete could answer, Joey shoved him hard with both hands.

"Look out, Pete!" Pam cried. Her brother teetered backward toward the librarian's desk on which stood several piles of books.

"Be careful!" Miss Allen cried out, rising from her chair.

But Pete could not regain his balance. He hit the side of the desk and fell, sending books flying through the air. One of the volumes skidded across Miss Allen's desk. It knocked her bottle of black drawing ink to the floor with a crash. A gasp arose from the onlookers.

"Are you hurt, Pete?" his sister asked anxiously.

"I'm all right."

By the time Pete picked himself up, however, a large pool of ink had spread over the floor near the librarian's desk.

"Look what Pete Hollister did!" Joey said triumphantly.

Miss Allen was not fooled! "It was just as much your fault as his, Joey Brill!" she told him.

"I'm sorry," Pete told the librarian. "I'll clean it up, Miss Allen."

"And Joey will help you," the woman declared. "You'll find a bucket and some cloths in the hall closet."

"I don't want to help *him*," Joey said sulkily. But

"Be careful!" Miss Allen cried out.

the librarian's stern look told the bully he had no other choice.

Together, he and Pete went into the hall and returned a few minutes later with a bucket of warm, sudsy water and several cleaning cloths. Together, they mopped up the ink, then started to rub out the stains.

"One thing I don't like to do is scrub floors!" Joey complained.

Pete made no comment and went about his task cheerfully. This angered Joey all the more.

"I'll get even with you for this," Joey said between clenched teeth, as they finished their work.

"You don't scare me," Pete replied.

Miss Allen told the boys they had done a good job, and added, "But don't fight in the library again. Joey, take the bucket to the janitor's room and dump it in the basin." The bully muttered a protest under his breath, but took the bucket and disappeared from the room.

At the same time a man walked into the library. He was short, slender, and well dressed. Pam noticed immediately that he had a slightly Oriental look to his eyes.

The stranger went straight to Miss Allen's desk, bowed politely, and in a soft voice, said, "I hear you have a book about secret New York tunnels on sale here. I should like to purchase it."

"We did have such a book," the librarian replied, "but I'm afraid you're too late. Pete Hollister bought it only a few moments ago."

The man turned and surveyed the room in one sweeping glance. "Which boy is Pete Hollister?"

"I am, sir," Pete said, stepping forward. He had an uneasy feeling as the man's eyes looked him over and then came to rest on the volume in his hand.

"I want that book on secret New York tunnels," the man said. "I'll pay you five dollars for it."

"Five dollars!" Pam exclaimed in amazement. "It cost my brother only twenty-five cents."

"Never mind that," the stranger went on. "I'm prepared to give you five dollars for it." He reached into his pocket and pulled out a wallet, removing a crisp bill from the fold. He held it out toward Pete. "Here you are," he said. "Now I'll take the book."

Pete did not accept the money. He looked first at his sister, then at the librarian. He did not know what to do. If the book were worth five dollars to this man, Pete thought, there must be a special reason. Could it be the mysterious note tucked among the pages?

Pete drew a deep breath and said, "I don't want to sell the book."

A silence followed as all the children waited to see what the man would do. A forced smile came over the fellow's face. He turned to Pam. "Please tell your brother not to be so foolish as to refuse my offer."

Pam did not hesitate. Her reply seemed to shock the Oriental-looking stranger. "I don't think Pete should sell it either."

At this moment Joey came back into the room and hurried forward to see what was going on. Learning of Pete's refusal to make such a tremendous profit, he said, "How stupid can you be, Pete?"

The Hollisters paid no attention to him.

"For the last time," the man said, a note of impatience in his voice, "I'll give you five dollars for the book!" He thrust the bill at Pete again.

"No, thank you."

The man flushed with anger and a piercing look came into his eyes. He slapped the money into his wallet.

"You'll be sorry," he said as he strode toward the door. "You'll regret that you didn't sell me that book! Wait and see what happens!"

CHAPTER 2

A CHOPSTICK MISHAP

As the stranger left the school library, the room buzzed with excited chatter.

"Good for you, Pete!"

"You did the right thing!"

"Maybe that book's worth a hundred dollars!"

Friends of the Hollisters continued to champion Pete's actions and even Miss Allen thought that the man had been rude and overbearing.

Joey did not agree. "I think anybody who wouldn't take five dollars for an old book is a dope," he said, and walked off.

Pete and Pam stayed long enough to buy a story book for each of their sisters, Sue and Holly, and their brother Ricky. Then, after wishing Miss Allen a happy vacation, they ran out of the school.

Reaching the front steps, they glanced about for the Oriental stranger. He was not in sight. But on the sidewalk Pam saw a small object glinting in the late morning sunlight. It was a bright red book of matches. She picked it up.

When Pam read the advertisement on the cover, she gasped. "Look, Pete!" Printed in black letters edged with gold were the words: LOTUS BLOSSOM RESTAURANT, CHINATOWN'S FINEST, NEW YORK CITY.

"Crickets!" Pete exclaimed. "I'll bet that man

dropped it. He must be Chinese and come from New York City."

"You mean he came all the way to Shoreham just to buy this old book about tunnels?" Pam asked.

"Maybe," Pete said. "The book or the letter may be very valuable."

The brother and sister turned the corner and hurried on. Pam said questioningly, "What I can't understand is how he knew the book was on sale at our school."

"Perhaps the person who contributed it told him," Pete replied.

Pam agreed this was possible. At the end of every school year the pupils collected used volumes from people all over town. Then, with the money made at the sale, new books were purchased for the school library.

"Perhaps Mother will have a suggestion about what to do next," Pam said as the Hollisters turned off the road and walked into their driveway.

The Hollister house, a large, comfortable, frame building, stood back from the road. The rear yard bordered beautiful Pine Lake.

"Mother is probably working in the garden," Pete said as they hurried along the side of the house.

"Hi, Mother!" Pam called out.

"Hello, dear," came the reply. Mrs. Hollister, a slim, pretty woman with blond hair was setting out snapdragon plants in her garden. She wore slacks, a plaid shirt, white cotton garden gloves, and a floppy wide-brimmed hat.

Near by were the three other Hollister children. Ricky, seven years old, was cultivating a row of newly-sprouted lima beans. He had tousled red hair and freckles that looked as if someone had dropped poppy seeds on his nose.

Holly, six, was mounding soil around the stems of a dozen hardy tomato plants. She, too, was dressed in jeans, and the manner in which she handled the hoe indicated she was used to gardening.

Kneeling on the ground near her was dark-haired Sue. She was four. In one hand Sue held a tin can, into which she was depositing worms which Holly had brought to the surface.

As Pete and Pam ran up to their mother, Mrs. Hollister asked gaily, "How was the book sale?"

"Great!" Pete answered. "We bought books for everybody."

"Goody!" said Sue.

"But best of all is a book on secret New York tunnels," Pete said, "and it has a mysterious message inside."

"Really?"

"Yes, a mystery!" Pam said. "What do you make of this, Mother?" She held the note toward Mrs. Hollister, who removed her garden gloves and looked at the writing.

"Where did you find this?" she asked.

Pam quickly told the story about the purchase of the book and the intrusion of the unpleasant stranger.

"Yikes!" Ricky exclaimed, dropping his cultivator

and running over to Pam's side. "Another mystery to solve. Oh, boy!"

"But we can't read this Japanese, or Chinese or whatever it is," said Mrs. Hollister, disappointed.

Sue had not been paying much attention until she heard the word "Chinese." Then she set the can of worms down for her friends the robins to eat. She walked over to Pam, wiping her grimy hands on her jeans. "I know who can read Chinese," she said.

"Who?" Ricky demanded.

"Norma's mother and father."

"That's right!" exclaimed Mrs. Hollister. "Norma Chen."

"She's in my nursery school class, and she's smart too," Sue remarked, feeling very important.

Norma, a black-haired, dark-eyed little girl, was the daughter of Mr. and Mrs. Sam Chen, who ran the Pagoda Restaurant in Shoreham. They were friendly, industrious, and well liked in the community.

Pam looked proudly at her sister. "Good idea, Susie," she said, and then added, "Come on, we'll all go to Mr. Chen's place and have him look at the note. If it's in Chinese, perhaps he can translate it."

"I'm certain he'll help you if he can," Mrs. Hollister said. She handed the note back to Pam and took the four books Pete and Pam had purchased.

The five children started across the lawn when suddenly their mother called out, "Pete! Ricky! I just remembered. Dad telephoned. He said that you boys were to come to *The Trading Post* as soon as Pete returned."

"What's up?" Pete asked.

"It's a secret." Mrs. Hollister's eyes twinkled.

Pete grinned. "Let's go, Ricky."

It was agreed that the three girls should call on the Chens to have the note translated while the boys went to *The Trading Post*. This was Mr. Hollister's combination hardware, sporting goods, and toy shop which was in the center of town. Pete and Ricky scooted off.

Meanwhile, the girls had run ahead. Fifteen minutes later they arrived at Mr. Chen's restaurant. It was not far from *The Trading Post*. They opened the door and walked in. A few diners were seated in bamboo chairs around small tables.

"Mm, some kind of food smells good. I'll bet it's chow mein," Pam remarked as a waiter stepped out from the kitchen.

He was a short man with a round, full face and a broad smile. "You like Chinese lunch?" he said. "Chow mein like this?"

"No, thank you," Pam replied. "We're looking for Mr. Chen."

"Mr. Chen not in right now," the waiter said haltingly.

"I want to see Norma," Sue spoke up. The waiter grinned even more broadly. "You friend of Norma?" he asked. "She lives next door in Chen apartment." The waiter pointed.

"Thank you," Holly said, and the three hurried outside and went next door.

The adjoining building had apartments upstairs and down. Pam read the names on the mailboxes and found that the Chens lived on the second floor. The girls walked up and knocked on the door. It was opened by a friendly-looking Chinese woman, whose black hair was pulled up into a knot at the back of her head.

"How do you do, Mrs. Chen," said Sue, acting very grown up. "I brought my sisters."

"I'm glad to see you," the woman smiled. "You wish to play with Norma?"

"Not exactly," Pam replied honestly. "We have a note written in an Oriental language, Mrs. Chen. We wonder whether it's in Chinese and if you can translate it for us."

"Step in, step in," Mrs. Chen invited. The girls did so and she closed the door behind them.

"Hello, Sue," said a bright-eyed little girl who skipped into the living room.

"Hello, Norma," Sue replied. "How's your finger painting?"

Norma rocked back and forth on one foot and looked sheepishly at her mother.

"Norma's doing fine with her finger painting," Mrs. Chen said, smiling. "Except I wish she wouldn't do it on the walls of her bedroom."

"Not any more, Mommy," Norma promised, and giggled.

"Please be seated," Mrs. Chen said, and nodded toward a nearby sofa.

Pam gave her the note. "Do you know what it says, Mrs. Chen?" she asked.

The woman read it slowly. "It's in Chinese," she said. "But——"

"But what?" Holly asked eagerly.

Mrs. Chen smiled. "Before I can reveal the contents, I would like to show this to my husband."

The Hollisters wondered why, but figured perhaps it is a custom for a Chinese wife to consult her husband before giving information.

"All right," Pam said. "May we wait for him, Mrs. Chen?"

"Of course, and while you are here, please stay to lunch with us."

"We'd like to," Pam said. "I'll have to telephone Mother and let her know where we are."

Mrs. Chen showed Pam to the telephone in the hall, and Mrs. Hollister readily assented to their staying for luncheon. While the Chinese woman prepared the meal, the four girls played together in the living room.

"Luncheon is served," came Mrs. Chen's cheerful voice from the dining room. The children took their seats at the table.

"Oh, goody," Norma said. "We're having pork and Chinese vegetables."

"Would you like to eat with chopsticks?" Mrs. Chen asked her guests.

"Oh, yes," Holly said. "That would be fun."

Their hostess provided each of the children with a pair of chopsticks.

"How do you use them?" Sue asked.

"Watch me," Mrs. Chen said kindly, as she held the chopsticks between the fingers of her right hand and deftly lifted morsels of food to her mouth.

The thin slices of pork and the savory vegetables were not too hard for the visitors to manage. But the rice was another matter. Poor Sue tried over and over again to make a portion of rice stay on her sticks long enough to get it to her mouth. But each time the food would drop off. Determined, she held the sticks almost parallel and finally managed to lift a ball of the rice.

"This time it's going to work," Sue told herself, opening her mouth and clutching the chopsticks tightly.

Then suddenly one of the sticks moved out of position. It crossed the other and *whoosh!* the rice flew up and landed in the little girl's hair!

"Oh, dear!" Pam cried out. Holly and Norma giggled.

Mrs. Chen quickly went for a towel and removed the bits of rice from Sue's black bangs and the top of her head. Then she handed Sue a spoon. "Perhaps you'd better eat the rice with this," she suggested kindly.

"Thank you," Sue answered. "I guess I'll need more practice to be a Chinese girl."

"I like Chinese food," said Holly when Mrs. Chen was again seated at the table. "I especially like these

The rice flew up and landed in Sue's hair.

little things. What are they?" she asked, as she held a slender white vegetable in her chopsticks.

"That's a bean sprout," Mrs. Chen replied.

"Oh," Sue remarked, "the poor little bean never had a chance to grow up, did it?"

As the luncheon went on, Pam told Mrs. Chen about the book which Pete had bought at the sale.

The Chinese woman looked very surprised. "What a coincidence!" she said. "I contributed that book to the school sale."

"Really?" Pam was so amazed she laid down her chopsticks.

Mrs. Chen told the girls that the book had been left in the restaurant by a customer a couple of years before. He had never come back for it.

"So I thought I'd send it to the book sale," she said, then added thoughtfully, "Something happened here this morning which was most unusual."

Mrs. Chen went on to say that a man had appeared at the restaurant a few hours before. He seemed to be partly Chinese.

"The man asked me for that very book on New York tunnels," the woman said.

"What did you do then?" Pam asked her.

"I directed him to the sale."

Just then the door opened and a stout Chinese gentleman stepped in.

"Oh, Daddy!" Norma called out. "We have company!"

Mr. Chen shook hands as he was introduced to

26

the Hollister girls. Then his wife spoke to him rapidly in Chinese and handed him the note. Mr. Chen read it several times as Pam, Holly, and Sue watched him intently. A strange look came over Mr. Chen's face.

CHAPTER 3

YOUNG DETECTIVES' KIT

"Please, what does the note say, Mr. Chen?" Pam asked, unable to restrain her curiosity.

The Chinese man shook his head. "This note was written in New York by a Yuen Foo to his son. It tells about Foo's proposed trip back to China thirteen years ago and the Father's worry that he might not return."

"What about the word 'Help'?" Pam wanted to know.

"That I cannot understand," Mr. Chen admitted as he handed the note back.

"Thank you so much, Mr. Chen," Pam said, as she and her sisters prepared to leave. "Pete and I thought the message might be something very important."

"It may be," the Chinese said. "And I hope you find the answer. I'm sorry I can't help you."

After thanking their hostess again for the delicious luncheon, the girls left Norma Chen's house. As they walked along the street toward home, Pam felt sure the strange letter contained a deep mystery. If she could only solve it! The Hollisters had solved mysteries ever since they had come to Shoreham, and had become known as good young detectives.

When the girls were near a corner, halfway home, they saw a car pull up to the curb right next to them and stop. A man stepped out.

Pam gasped in surprise. He was the same person who had wanted to buy their book at the library sale!

Noticing that Pam looked worried, the stranger said, "Don't be afraid of me, miss."

"I—I'm not," Pam stammered, as she held Sue and Holly tightly by the hand.

"All I want is the book about the tunnels," the man went on earnestly.

"I don't have it with me," Pam said, trying to put him off. "It's at home."

The stranger looked so disappointed that for a moment Pam felt sorry for him. "Why do you want the book so badly?" she asked.

Instantly the man's face brightened. "Honestly, I can say it is not the book which I seek," he said, "but there is a note in it giving a secret recipe for Bird's Nest Soup."

Holly giggled in spite of herself. "Bird's Nest Soup? You really mean it?"

"Oh, yes," the man went on. He told them that a certain kind of swallow builds its nest on the cliffs near the south coast of China. "The birds catch fish," he explained, "and store bits of it in the nests so that the baby birds will always have a supply of food.

"Natives gather the birds' nests and use them to make a delicious soup," he continued. The stranger smiled and added, "That's why I'm here in Shoreham."

Holly spoke up. "But we don't have any birds' nests here for making soup."

"No. Instead you have an old recipe left by my

uncle, who was a famous chef. He put it in a book, which unfortunately was left at a restaurant here in Shoreham. I have traced the recipe a long way, and now——" He spread his hands apart in a gesture of discouragement.

The man's story made Pam's sympathy turn to suspicion. If Mr. Chen had translated the note correctly, this man was not telling the truth. The girl decided to test the stranger's honesty. Reaching into her pocket she pulled out the note, opened it, and held it toward him. "Is this the recipe?" she asked.

The man's dark eyes moved quickly over the paper. Then he grinned broadly. "Yes, this is it."

As he reached for the note, Pam shoved it quickly into her pocket again and stepped back. At the same time Holly blurted out, "That isn't a recipe. We know what it says."

The stranger looked angry. He glanced up and down the street. Then he stepped toward Pam as if to try snatching the note away from her. But to her relief she saw Pete and Ricky run around the corner toward them. Pete had a package under his arm.

"Hurry!" Holly called out to them frantically.

The man, seeing the boys, retreated to his car. He opened the door, jumped in and drove off. As he did Pam made a mental note of the New York state license number.

"Hey, what's going on here?" Pete asked, reaching the girls.

Pam quickly brought her brothers up to date on what had happened.

30

"Isn't this kit a beauty?" Pete asked.

"Crickets!" Pete exclaimed. "I wonder what his game is?"

"He certainly doesn't want any recipe," Pam said emphatically.

"Of course not," Pete agreed. "But why is he so eager to get Yuen Foo's note?"

"What's that you have under your arm?" Holly asked as she looked at the large package.

Pete winked at his brother and said, "It's a present from Dad. Something new he wants to sell at the store. He would like us to try it out first."

The children sat down on the curb, and Pete tore the brown paper off the package. Inside was a play box marked Junior Detective Kit. Pete opened it. "Isn't this a beauty?" he asked Pam.

"Wonderful!" the girl replied. The box contained a fingerprint outfit, chemicals to show up invisible ink, and a set of handcuffs.

"Boy, will we be able to do some detective work with this!" Ricky said importantly. "We'll be able to outfox everybody."

Pam eagerly began to read the instructions on the fingerprint outfit. As she was busily doing this two boys came down the street on bicycles.

"Oh, oh," Holly remarked. "Here come Joey and Will."

Will Wilson was a pal of Joey's and spent much of his free time playing with the bully. Left alone, Will did not get into much mischief, but with Joey as a pal he seemed to be in trouble most of the time.

"Make believe we don't see them," Pam advised as the two boys rode up.

But Joey and Will stopped. They steadied their bikes with one foot against the curb.

"What have you got there?" Joey asked.

"Just a game," Pete remarked.

"Oh, yes?" Will put in. "What kind of a game is it?"

"Please go away and don't bother us," Pam requested.

A half smile came to Joey's lips. "Don't be sore because I beat your brother this morning," he said scornfully.

"You didn't beat anybody!" Pam spoke up hotly.

"Oh, well," Joey shrugged, "who wanted your silly looking old note anyhow?"

Instead of going away, however, Joey and Will lowered the kick stands of their bicycles, and came closer to the Hollisters.

"Aw, don't be afraid to show us your game," Joey begged.

"We won't make any trouble," Will added.

"You'd better not," Pete said determinedly.

By now the two bullies had read the name on the box containing the junior detective kit. "Say, that's real keen!" Joey said. "Did you get it at your father's store?"

"Yes. Dad's going to sell them, maybe."

Pete held the box at arm's length and let the two boys see the contents. Joey was most intrigued by the handcuffs.

"Gee, I'd like to examine them," he said. "Won't you let me?"

Pete felt that if he let Joey play with the handcuffs for a while, it might mean a future sale of a detective kit at *The Trading Post* if his father decided to stock them.

"All right," he agreed finally. "I'll let you try the cuffs, if you promise not to break them."

"Okay, I promise," Joey said. Pete handed him the handcuffs and the key with which to unlock them.

Joey and Will walked off a few paces, clicking and unclicking the handcuffs open and shut. Meanwhile, Pete and Pam, with Sue and Holly looking on, were reading instructions for the rest of the outfit. Ricky wandered over to see what Joey and Will were doing.

"Come here, Ricky," Joey said in a low voice. "Will and I have a little bet."

"What's that?" Ricky asked.

"Will doesn't think you can get your arms around that electric light pole over there."

"No, he can't," Will spoke up.

"But I say he can," remarked Joey, thrusting his chin forward. "I think Ricky is getting to be a pretty big fellow."

Ricky glanced over at the metal street light pole. He threw out his chest proudly. "Sure I can get my arms around that old light pole," he declared. "I'll show you."

"What did I tell you?" Joey said as the three boys walked over to the curb.

Pete and Pam were so intent upon reading the instructions in the box that they did not notice Ricky putting his arms around the metal pole. But as he did, Joey quickly grasped the younger boy by the wrists.

Click, click! The handcuffs had him caught!

"Hey, fellows, what are you doing?" Ricky asked, surprised. He struggled to free himself. "Let me go! Unlock the handcuffs!" he demanded.

Joey and Will stood back, laughing at the boy's predicament. "Ha, ha!" Joey guffawed. "Now we're even with you."

As Ricky cried out, his brother and sisters glanced up from the instructions they were reading.

"Joey," said Pete sternly, "you promised not to make any trouble."

"I did not!" the bully retorted. "I only said I wouldn't break your old game, and I haven't."

"Unlock Ricky!" Pam demanded.

"Yes, please," the prisoner exclaimed. "This isn't any fun."

"Unlock him yourself," Will taunted as Joey thrust the key into his pocket.

Handing the detective kit to Holly, Pete and Pam leaped up and ran toward Joey and Will. "Give us the key!" cried Pete.

The two bullies sprang onto their bicycles and pedaled off furiously. Pete gained on Will and tried to grasp his rear mudguard, but fell short and tumbled into the street. By the time he picked himself up

Joey and Will had sped around the corner and were far down the street.

Ricky, meanwhile, still struggled to free himself. "Ow! Help!" he cried out. "This hurts!"

CHAPTER 4

SECRET WRITING

Pete tried to pull the handcuffs apart and free Ricky, but he could not budge them. Pam and Holly tried too, but with no better results.

"One thing is sure," said Pete. "These are good handcuffs."

"*Too* good," Ricky complained. "Yikes! Can't you get me out? My arms hurt."

"Oh dear!" Sue wailed. "Maybe poor Ricky will have to stay here all night."

"No, he won't!" Pam declared hopefully. "We'll unlock him somehow!"

It was decided that Pete would hurry to *The Trading Post* and get a handcuff key from another detective kit. While Sue, Holly, and Pam stayed with Ricky, Pete set off at a brisk trot.

A few minutes later he arrived at *The Trading Post* out of breath. Pete opened the door and ran inside the modern-looking store. His father stood at one side near the toy counter talking to another man. Mr. Hollister, dark-haired, tall and good-looking, was amazed to see his son returning so soon.

Pete raced up to him. "Ricky's handcuffed, Dad!"

His father grinned. "I guess that's what the handcuffs are for, son. What's all the excitement about?"

Pete quickly told his father what had happened. "I'll get you a duplicate key," Mr. Hollister said. He leaned over the toy counter and picked up another kit.

Opening the box, he gave Pete the key out of it. Then he spoke to the other man. "Mr. Davis, I'd like you to meet my son Pete."

Mr. Davis smiled and shook hands with the boy. He was a short, stocky man with black hair graying at the temples. Mr. Davis had a pleasant smile and Pete liked him immediately. "How do you do, sir," the boy said.

Mr. Hollister explained that Mr. Davis was an old friend of his, a toy manufacturer from New York City.

"Yes," the toy man said, smiling, "I have an idea to talk over with your dad. I value his opinion. But first, let me drive you back to your brother."

"Thank you! Good-by, Dad."

Pete hurried out of the store with Mr. Davis, whose car was parked at the curb. A few minutes later they pulled up to the light pole which Ricky was hugging like a monkey on a stick.

"Sure was a mean trick for those fellows to run away and leave your brother there," Mr. Davis sympathized as he stopped the car. Pete jumped out with the key and quickly unlocked his handcuffed brother.

"Yikes! Joey sure pulled a fast one on me," Ricky laughed, and began rubbing his arms vigorously. Pete then introduced his sisters and brother to Mr. Davis.

At that moment their attention was diverted by the sound of a siren far down the street. A police car sped up, parked behind Mr. Davis's automobile and a handsome young man in uniform stepped out.

38

"It sure was a mean trick to handcuff you."

"Officer Cal!" the Hollisters exclaimed. Sue ran up and threw her arms about him.

Cal Newberry was an old friend of the Hollisters and had helped them solve several mysteries. Cal and Mr. Davis exchanged nods, and the policeman said, "Hi, kids! What's the excitement?"

When Pete told him about Joey's trick, Officer Cal said, "So that's it! A woman driving past reported that a small boy was fastened to a light pole. Well, I'm glad you got loose. I'll get that key back from Joey Brill."

"Thank you, Officer Cal," Pam said. "But before you go, perhaps you can help us with a new mystery we just came upon."

The policeman grinned broadly. "Another mystery, you say? What's this one about?"

"Chinatown in New York!" Ricky declared.

"An interesting place," Mr. Davis said.

"It sounds exciting," the policeman went on. "Tell me about it."

Pam related all that had happened, finally adding, "I remember the license number of the car." She told Officer Cal and he jotted it down on a pad.

"I can find out who this stranger is," he said, "but it doesn't sound as though he has done anything to break the law so far."

With a smart salute Officer Cal stepped into the police car. The policeman waved to the children and promised, "If I locate this man, I'll keep an eye on him for you."

With that Cal drove off and Mr. Davis said to the

Hollisters, "Hop in my car and I'll take you home."

"Thanks a lot!" Pete said and they all clambered in.

On the way the toy manufacturer told them about his mission to Shoreham. "I have a new toy," he explained, "called the Soaring Satellite. I dropped in to ask your dad's opinion of it."

"Does it sail into outer space?" Ricky asked.

The toy man laughed. "The Soaring Satellite doesn't quite go into outer space," he said with a chuckle. "As a matter of fact, it's not yet perfected."

"Please tell us about it," Pete pleaded eagerly.

Mr. Davis said that the new toy—he was sorry he did not have a model with him—consisted of a large balloon with a metallic track around the circumference. It also had a small toy rocket and an electronic control box.

"The balloon is a make-believe moon," he went on. "The track around it is the orbit for the rocket, which is the satellite."

"That sounds keen!" Ricky exclaimed. "How does it work?"

The toy manufacturer replied that the satellite was launched electrically, then it soared into orbit around the make-believe moon. "A child can operate the control box," he said, "making the satellite go round and round."

"I'm sure Dad could sell plenty of them!" Pete declared.

As they neared the Hollister home, Mr. Davis continued, "I was about to ask your father to come to

New York City to see the first tryout of the Soaring Satellite. How would you all like to come and visit my office in the Empire State Building?"

"Yikes!" Ricky said. "Sure, we'd love to come."

"You'd enjoy a trip to the skyscraper city," Mr. Davis remarked, smiling. "And while you're there you can see the Soaring Satellite on display at the Hobby Show in the Coliseum."

The car stopped in front of the Hollisters' home and the children got out. All said they certainly would like to make the trip to New York.

"And thank you for the ride, Mr. Davis," Pam said.

The children rushed into the house to tell their mother about the mysterious stranger and Mr. Davis's invitation to visit the big city. Then, while Pete showed Mrs. Hollister the new junior detective kit, Sue and Holly wandered out into the garden.

A few minutes later Ricky followed them. He found the girls bending over the row of sprouting beans. Sue held a saucepan in her hands while Holly pulled up the tender young shoots and dropped them into it.

"Say, what are you doing?" Ricky asked them.

"We—we're digging bean sprouts," Holly answered.

"But why?"

"It's a secret," Sue continued. "We can't tell you. And don't you dare tell anybody else. This is for Mother's surprise." They refused to say anything further.

Ricky looked at his sisters. "You'd better plant

some more seeds right away. I'll get them for you."

He hurried into the house for a packet of seeds. Holly put them in a row and covered them with soil. Sue patted the earth firmly.

As Ricky strolled off, wondering what the surprise was, Holly went for a watering can. She filled it at a faucet extending from the side of the house. The two sisters grasped the handle and carried the water to the garden and sprinkled the seeds.

"There'll be more bean sprouts in a few days," Holly said. "And I'm sure Mother will be happy with our surprise."

"Shall we go right away?"

"Yes. It'll take a while."

Sue glanced over to the back steps, where White Nose, the family cat, was playing with her five kittens, Midnight, Snowball, Tutti Frutti, Smokey, and Cuddly. The little girl stopped to pick up Cuddly and held the kitten under her left arm like a purse.

"I'll take you along," she said.

"Hurry, Sue," Holly urged. She stood on the sidewalk with the pan of bean sprouts in her hands. Sue skipped to her sister's side and together the girls hurried down the street.

Pete and Pam, meanwhile, were in the house looking over the junior detective kit and at the same time pondering the cryptic Chinese message and why it was in the book.

"The note seems to be innocent enough," Pam observed, "but I feel that the word 'help' has a special

43

meaning. Maybe it was a code word between Yuen Foo and his son."

At this remark Pete snapped his fingers. "I have it, Pam!" he exclaimed. "Maybe there's a hidden message in the note. I'll test it with the chemicals from our detective kit."

His sister was excited over the idea. Taking the kit into the kitchen, they put it on the table, then got a soup bowl from the closet. In the bowl they mixed two of the chemicals according to directions.

"Here goes the note," Pete said tensely as he put the white paper into the mixture. The sheet became thoroughly wet and settled to the bottom of the bowl. Pete and Pam gazed at it intently for a few moments. Nothing happened.

"I guess I was wrong." Pete gave a sigh of disappointment.

"Wait!" Pam pointed excitedly. "Look, Pete! Some new letters are appearing beside the first ones!"

As if by magic two additional lines of Chinese characters stood out faintly on the paper!

CHAPTER 5

THE EAVESDROPPER

"A secret message!" Pete cried out as the symbols on the mysterious note grew bold and black in the liquid.

"You were right!" Pam declared. "Oh, Pete, we must find out right away what it says."

Hearing their excited shouts, Mrs. Hollister hastened into the kitchen.

"Pete solved part of the mystery with his detective chemicals!" Pam's eyes were alight, as she lifted the damp paper out and showed it to her mother.

"This is amazing," Mrs. Hollister agreed.

Pam chuckled. "I'm sure it's not a recipe for Bird's Nest Soup!"

Pete quickly dried the moist paper with a blotter. "We'll take it to Mr. Chen at once for translation," he proposed.

By now Ricky had come into the house and was as curious as his older brother and sister. "Let me go with you, please," he begged.

The three children hurried off. They were fairly bursting with curiosity to hear the translation by the time they reached Mr. Chen's restaurant. They found him seated at a table, working an abacus with amazing speed. Behind him near a partly opened window stood an ornate stand with a large beautiful Oriental vase on it.

When Pam introduced Pete and Ricky, Mr. Chen

looked up from his counting board and smiled. "You have found another note in the old book?"

"No, Mr. Chen, it's the same note, but with a new message." Pete explained and handed the limp paper to the Chinese.

"You are very good detectives," he told them, and began to read the message.

The restaurant man scanned it several times with no change of expression on his placid countenance. Then his eyes lifted slowly from the paper to the children standing before him.

"This is truly a Chinese mystery," he said. "And it may be a very dangerous one."

The Hollisters stared in astonishment. *Dangerous!* They looked at one another and were silent for a few moments.

Then Pam said, "Please tell us the translation."

Mr. Chen shook his head. "Maybe I should not," he answered, as he tapped the counting board with his fingers. "I would not want to see you get into trouble."

"We won't!" Ricky assured him eagerly.

"Are you sure you want me to translate it for you?" Mr. Chen asked gravely.

"Oh yes!" said Pete. "We'll promise to be very careful."

"I hope so," came the reply. "And now I will read it to you."

The three children held their breaths while Mr. Chen translated the new words. "Honorable son: I am in great danger and am threatened because I have the treasure. However, it is safely guarded by Kuan Yen. My enemies will never find the great bird."

There was silence for a moment after Mr. Chen had finished reading. Pete gave a long sigh. "This mystery is getting deeper. Who is Kuan Yen, I wonder?"

Mr. Chen explained that Kuan Yen was the Chinese goddess of mercy. "Many of my people have a statue of her in their homes."

After a pause he added, "My good little friends, why don't you forget about this mystery? Not only is it dangerous, but it happened many years ago. Yuen Foo, who wrote the letter, is probably not in trouble any more."

Pam was not convinced. "But Mr. Chen," she said, "why is this stranger in town so interested in getting the message if it was written so long ago?"

"Yes," Pete spoke up. "Maybe Yuen Foo *is* in trouble right now."

The Chinese restaurant man smiled slowly, a far-away look coming into his eyes. "And how can you hope to find Yuen Foo?" he asked. "New York is a long distance off."

"That's true," Pete said, "but we've all been invited to come to the city and see Mr. Davis's new Soaring Satellite."

"Soaring Satellite?" Mr. Chen looked unbelievingly at the children. "Surely you're not planning to fly to the moon?"

"Oh, no." Ricky grinned. "It's just a toy," and told their Chinese friend about it.

"If we go to New York to see the Soaring Satellite," Pete said, "maybe we can work on the mystery too."

"But if you do, be very —— —"

"Look!" Ricky shouted suddenly. He pointed to a partly opened window behind Mr. Chen. The figure of a man had suddenly appeared and then vanished.

"An eavesdropper!" Pam cried out. "He was trying to hear what we're saying!"

Ricky dashed toward the window from one side and Pete the other. In Pete's path was the large Chinese vase. He thought he had dodged around it, but his elbow banged into the vase. It teetered and crashed to the floor.

"Oh!" Pete groaned, looking down at the pieces of broken pottery. "I'm so sorry!"

"Do not worry about it," Mr. Chen said kindly. "Who was at the window?"

Quickly Ricky looked out, but could see no one. "Maybe the fellow ducked around back," the boy suggested.

With that, the three children hurried out of the restaurant and dashed down an alley to the side of the building. Nobody was there.

Ricky ran into the back yard. It was a small enclosure with a green lawn, two dogwood trees in the center and a row of iris along a board fence at the rear. Ricky ran to it and saw two deep footprints in the soft dirt. "Pete! Pam!" he called.

"If we hurry, we can catch the prowler!"

As his sister and brother ran up, there came a series of barks and howls from the yard beyond.

"That must be from the kennel at the back of Jack's Pet Shoppe," said Pam.

Ricky pointed out the footprints and Pete said, "Somebody vaulted the fence here. If we hurry, we can catch up to the prowler!"

He put a leg over the fence and dropped to the other side, careful not to step on any of the kennel runs. Ricky did the same. The animals set up a fearful din. Pam said she would stay behind and watch in case the fellow should show up from some other direction.

"Okay, follow me Rick," Pete commanded as he pushed his way along the edge of the kennels. But when he came to the rear of the pet shop, a woman cried out from the doorway, "Stay where you are! Don't move another step!"

Both boys were startled by her sharp voice. "We're chasing somebody," Pete said somewhat lamely.

"We have to catch him!" Ricky declared, and started for the alley which led to the street.

"No you don't!" the woman shouted. "I saw your friend jump the fence. He frightened my dogs."

"Please," Pete said, "that fellow isn't our friend."

"Then why are you playing games with him?"

Pete sighed, shrugged and looked at Ricky. It seemed impossible to explain.

"Now go right back where you came from," she added acidly. "This is private property—and be careful of my dogs!"

Realizing that they were trespassing, although harmlessly and for a good cause, Pete obeyed. Ricky, frowning, followed his brother to the fence and hopped over, as the animals continued their howling.

Pam was waiting. "What a shame," she said. "If that woman had only let you go, you might have caught up with the eavesdropper."

"If he's trying to find out something, he'll be back," Pete prophesied. "So we may find out yet."

The disappointed children returned to Mr. Chen's restaurant. They told the proprietor of the prowler's escape. "Too bad," he said. "But then, he may not be connected with your mystery."

The Hollisters talked a little longer with Mr. Chen, who had disposed of the broken vase, then said they must leave.

"And please forgive me for breaking your vase," Pete said earnestly. "My dad will see you about it."

"Maybe," Pam spoke up, "we could buy you another in New York's Chinatown. We hope to go there."

Again, Mr. Chen told the Hollisters not to worry about the vase. "Real happiness," he said, "comes to a person from acts of friendship, not pieces of pottery."

The Chinese bowed and wished the children luck in solving the mystery. "But be careful, very careful," he cautioned.

Just then a wall telephone rang. Mr. Chen answered it and beckoned to Pam as she was leaving the restaurant. "Come back," he said. "It's for you."

Pam picked up the receiver. "Hello—oh, Mother." Then she listened for a moment. "Thank you, Mother. Good-by."

"What's the news?" Pete asked.

Pam said that Officer Cal had contacted the Hollister home. "That car we saw with the New York license belongs to a man named Hong Yee," she reported. "Mother thought you might know him, Mr. Chen."

"I have never heard the name before," the Chinese answered.

"Hong Yee lives in New York," Pam went on.

Since the restaurateur could give them no further information, the Hollisters said good-by again and started home. On the way they talked about the great bird mentioned in the hidden writing. Ricky thought perhaps it meant a large parrot, trained to guard valuables, by calling out when someone approached.

"Or, it could be a falcon," Pete said. "Falconry is an Oriental sport, you know."

"Maybe the bird itself is the treasure," Pam offered.

Ricky did not think so. "If it were," he said, jogging along, "it would be dead by this time."

After discussing all angles of the mysterious note, the three Hollisters arrived home. It was nearly time for supper, and they caught the tempting aroma of a delicious meat loaf their mother had prepared.

Pete, Pam, and Ricky hurried toward the kitchen

door to find Mrs. Hollister calling into the yard for Holly and Sue. "Have you seen them?" she asked the older children.

"No, Mother," replied Pam.

Zip, the Hollisters' lovely collie dog, sensing that the two younger girls were missing, began sniffing about the yard as if trying to pick up their scent.

"I wish I knew where those two went," Mrs. Hollister said. "They've been gone a long time and I'm worried."

"Perhaps they're hiding in the stall with Domingo, and are waiting for us to find them," Pete suggested.

He went to the large garage located at one side of the property and opened the door. Domingo, the family's pet burro, was standing in his stall on a pile of straw. The two girls were not there.

"Sue and Holly have been gone since shortly after you left," Mrs. Hollister said when Pete returned. "They didn't say where they were going." Her voice was edged with concern.

"We'll find them, Mother," Pam said reassuringly. "Don't worry."

She and Pete looked along the shore of Pine Lake, while Ricky trotted down the street, calling loudly. But after a fifteen minute search, Holly and Sue had not been found.

"Oh, dear, they are usually so prompt in coming home at supper time," Mrs. Hollister said nervously.

Just then the children's father arrived in the family station wagon.

"Have you seen Holly and Sue?" Mrs. Hollister questioned him hopefully.

"No. Is something wrong?" he asked.

"I'm afraid," Mrs. Hollister said fearfully, "that the girls may be lost!"

CHAPTER 6

TWO BULLIES AND A GHOST

Mr. Hollister took a more practical view of the girls' disappearance. "Have you phoned their playmates?" he asked.

"All but the Hunters," Mrs. Hollister replied. Jeff, eight, and his sister Ann, ten, were among the Hollisters' best friends.

Going into the house, Mrs. Hollister dialed the Hunter home. Mrs. Hunter answered. "No, Holly and Sue are not here. And my Ann has been gone for some time too. "I'm getting worried. The three girls may be together."

"But where?" Mrs. Hollister asked. Mrs. Hunter said she did not have the faintest idea, but would start a search.

When his mother hung up, Ricky said, "I know the girls were planning a surprise for you. And I saw Sue carry Cuddly off."

"That's very interesting, but how does it help us find the girls?" Mr. Hollister asked.

Pam had a suggestion. "Let's tell Zip to pick up their scent." She ran to get a shoe of Holly's and one of Sue's. "Now sniff these," she commanded the dog, "and then find the girls!"

The beautiful collie craned his neck toward the shoes. Then, with his nose to the ground, he sniffed about the yard for a minute, turned and started down the street. Pam and her mother hurried after him, while Pete, Ricky and their father searched in the opposite direction.

"Zip's going toward the Hunters' house," Pam said. "Holly and Sue came here. I guess Ann went off with them."

Zip continued on to the Hunters' back yard just as Mrs. Hunter came to join the Hollisters. The dog dashed among some rose bushes beside the big two-car garage. A kitten jumped out and scampered up a magnolia tree.

"Cuddly!" Pam exclaimed, and ran on ahead of the women. She reached up into the branches of the magnolia and retrieved the pet.

At the same time Zip began to paw on the closed garage door and whine.

"Goodness!" Mrs. Hunter exclaimed. "Do you suppose the girls have been in the garage all this time?"

Pam opened the door and Zip bounded inside. The sudden entrance startled three little girls who were busily working over a toy electric stove.

"Sue! Holly! Ann! So this is where you've been hiding!" Pam cried out.

"We're not really hiding," Holly spoke up. "Sue and I are making a supper surprise on Ann's stove."

Pretty, dark-haired Ann giggled. "You'll never guess what it is. Tell them, Sue."

"It's—it's Chinese. We call it Birds' House Chop Suey."

"What!" exclaimed Pam and the two women.

"It should have been Birds' Nest Soup, but we

"It's Bird's House Chop Suey," Sue said.

couldn't find a nice clean bird's nest," Holly explained.

"Mother's supposed to eat this?" Pam asked, gazing doubtfully into a small pot of food bubbling on the toy stove. "What's in it?"

Holly related how the girls had borrowed Mrs. Hollister's bean sprouts from the garden. When her mother gasped she quickly explained that they had planted other seeds. They had also obtained celery and onions from the Hollister kitchen. In addition, Ann had taken bits of pork sausage from the Hunters' refrigerator. They had chopped this up into the soup for flavor.

"And we added a dash of soy sauce too," Ann concluded with a knowing smile like that of a master chef.

"Why did you give it that funny name?" Pam asked. "Bird House Chop Suey."

For answer Holly fished a tiny twig out of the saucepan. Giggling, she said it had come from a dilapidated birdhouse in the magnolia tree.

"Ugh!" said Pam, making a wry face.

"We washed it very well," Sue spoke up.

"And I'm sure your special Chinese dish is delicious," said Mrs. Hollister, smiling. Lifting a spoonful to her mouth, she blew on the soup to cool it, then tasted some. "Very good. Mm. Very good."

"Even without the bird's nest?" Sue asked, pleased.

"Thank goodness you couldn't find one!" Mrs. Hollister said, laughing. "Come now, we must leave."

Using a small pot holder, she lifted the pan from the stove, poured some of the stew into a tiny bowl for the Hunters, then walked home with her children. Mr. Hollister and the boys returned, glad to see the girls.

They laughed heartily to hear about the Bird House Chop Suey which was served as a first course at supper by Holly and Sue.

Table talk that evening was mostly about the Chinese mystery. Mr. Hollister said he was glad that Officer Cal had taken part in tracing down the New York stranger.

Then while Mrs. Hollister served dessert of a sweet pink pudding, Pete asked if he might read aloud some interesting excerpts from his book on New York tunnels.

"We'd love to hear them," his mother replied.

"Here's a funny one," Pete said, opening the book. "Years ago a light pole on Amsterdam Avenue suddenly began to sink through the pavement. Police investigated and beneath it they found a man digging a tunnel from his home to a store across the street."

"Goodness!" Mrs. Hollister said. "Why did the man do that?"

"He was afraid of the street traffic!"

The Hollisters laughed merrily.

"And here's the spookiest story of all." Pete flipped the pages, found the spot he wanted, and read, "One time long ago, New York City officials came upon a long underground tunnel connecting two basement rooms on opposite sides of Mott Street in Chinatown.

They had been dug half a century before and it was said a skeleton used to walk back and forth through the tunnel. Anyway, the officials filled in the passageway."

Ricky's eyes glowed. "Yikes!" he exclaimed. "Tunnels in Chinatown! Do you suppose we could ever find a mystery like that?"

"I doubt it," Pete replied. "The book says that most of the private tunnels of New York have been filled. The city is so heavily built up that officials were afraid the streets might cave in."

"New York has enough tunnels as it is," Mr. Hollister added. He told about the many miles of subways and the large vehicular tunnels linking Manhattan Island with surrounding areas.

When supper was over and the girls were clearing the table, Officer Cal drove up in front of the Hollister home. They watched as he stepped out of the car, walked up the drive, and knocked on the door. Pete greeted him.

"Come in, Officer Cal," he said. "Any more news?"

The policeman doffed his cap and, as the others gathered around, told them that more information had arrived about Hong Yee.

"He's an importer," the policeman said. "Hong Yee specializes in jade jewelry." Then he added quickly, "I don't think you Hollisters will be bothered by him any more though."

"What do you mean?" Pam asked.

Cal said that the stranger, under surveillance by

the local police all day, had driven out of town and later the state police had reported that he had left the state.

"Then I suppose he's going back to New York," Pete surmised.

"If he was the eavesdropper at Mr. Chen's restaurant," Pam said a little fearfully, "perhaps he has learned the secret of the message and is headed back to Chinatown."

"That might be so," Cal agreed.

"Thank you," Mrs. Hollister said. "We'll feel much safer now that the fellow has left Shoreham."

A few moments after Cal had departed, the telephone rang. Pete answered it. The voice on the other end was soft and hissing. "This is your mysterious friend," it said.

Instantly Pete was suspicious. Was this Joey Brill up to one of his tricks? If so, Pete decided to play along with him. "I suppose you want the book," the boy responded.

"Yes. Leave it under the tree on the school playground at nine o'clock tonight, or else I will put a Chinese curse on you!"

Pete tried to sound frightened. "All right, I'll do it. Please don't put a curse on me!" He hung up and, chuckling, told his family what had happened. Then he added, "I'll turn the tables on Joey Brill!"

"How?" Ricky asked.

"Oh, I'll think of something."

Alone with his brother a few minutes later, Pete outlined his plan. When he had finished, Ricky remarked, "Boy, that'll be great. I wish I could see it, Pete."

"I'd better do it alone," the older brother replied. "But I'll tell you all how things turn out. First, lend me your water pistol, Ricky."

By eight o'clock that evening the sun had set, and long shadows began to throw a cloak of darkness over Shoreham. Pete loaded Ricky's water pistol and put it into his pants' pocket. Then he hurried to the school yard, went to the big tree, and shinned up to the topmost branches.

Thoroughly hidden by the thick foliage, Pete waited. Half an hour went by before he heard voices beneath him. Peering down through the leaves, he recognized Joey and Will. The latter was carrying a brown bag in his arms.

Joey climbed up to the first limb, then reached down to take the bag from his friend. Will shinned up and together the pair flattened themselves out on the limb and waited.

Pete watched for a while, chuckling to himself. Finally he heard Joey say, "It's almost nine o'clock. Won't Pete ever get here?"

"Shsh!" Will cautioned. "If he's coming he might hear you."

Quietly Pete pulled the water pistol from his pocket. Taking aim through the leaves, he squeezed the trigger.

Squirt!

"Hey, what's that?" Joey whispered.

"What's what?"

"Something hit my face. It feels like water!"

"You're dreamin'."

"I'm not dreamin'. Just hold that bag of mud and keep quiet."

Pete squeezed the trigger again.

"Wow, I felt it too!" Will said. "Right in my ear!"

Pete chuckled to himself and shook the top of the tree, making a mysterious rustling noise.

"Wh-what's that?" Will cried.

"A g-ghost," Joey quavered.

Now for the first time Pete spoke out. Using a high-pitched voice, he said, "You are spoiling plans of Chinese mandarin. I will catch you and feed you to the dragon!" He shook the top of the tree again, as though he were climbing down.

Joey and Will glanced up, terrified. "Hold the sack," Joey chattered, "until I jump down out of here." With that, he dropped to the ground.

But Will was trembling so much that his hands could not hold onto the bag tightly. He dropped it.

"Look out!" he cried.

Instead, Joey looked up. The mud bag hit him full in the face, breaking open with a soggy *plop*.

"Ow!" he bellowed. The bully spluttered and danced about as he wiped the mud out of his eyes. Will dropped from the limb beside his friend, and Pete shook the tree more violently.

"Let's get out of here!" Will whispered, and the two boys raced off faster than Pete had ever seen them go.

Now Pete laughed out loud and climbed down the

tree. He hurried home to tell Ricky what had happened. The brothers chuckled for the rest of the evening, and both went to sleep with happy smiles on their faces.

Next morning at breakfast, Mr. Hollister announced, "We're all going to New York to see the Soaring Satellite at the Hobby Show!"

"Yikes! Great."

"Oh, Daddy, you're wonderful!" Holly said, flinging her arms about him.

"And we can solve the Chinese mystery!" Pete remarked.

"And help poor old Yuen Foo," Pam added.

At noontime Mr. Hollister telephoned home to say that reservations had been made and airline tickets bought. After lunch, Pete called Dave Mead, his best friend, and asked if he would come over twice a day and look after Domingo.

"I'll be right over to see about it," his friend said.

Dave, a dark-haired, good-looking boy, rode his bicycle into the yard, hopped off and ran over to the garage where Pete was curry-combing the donkey.

"That's some trip you're going to take," Dave said, then added, "You certainly look happy."

"I am. For a couple of reasons," Pete replied, and told his friend about the episode the evening before.

"Wow, that's a riot!" Dave grinned. "Those two monkeys will never live that down!"

As Pete was instructing Dave on how to feed and exercise Domingo for the next few days, the boys glanced toward the street. They were just in time to see Joey and Will ride past on their bicycles.

"Hi, Joey!" Pete called out.

Joey put on his brakes and Will also stopped. Pete and Dave walked over to the curb, observing that the local mischief-makers seemed very subdued.

"What do you want?" Joey said in a disgruntled tone of voice.

"Oh, nothing important," Dave replied, "but I understand you spoiled the plan of a Chinese gentleman."

Suddenly a queer look came over Joey's face, which grew as red as a firecracker. "Wh-what? How do you know?"

As if in reply, Domingo lifted his head high in his stall and a plaintive hee-haw carried to the street. Pete and Dave roared with laughter. Without another word, Joey and Will raced off.

The rest of the day was spent in excited plans by the Hollisters for their trip to New York. The family was to leave late the next afternoon.

"I can't wait to go," Holly declared, and the others agreed.

Just before bedtime that evening, a telegram came for Mr. Hollister. The message caused the children to groan in dismay.

"Have run into trouble on Soaring Satellite. Not perfected yet. You may prefer postponing trip. Signed, Charlie Davis."

CHAPTER 7

TRICKS OF THE WIND

The Hollister family looked at one another in disappointment. Mr. Davis was suggesting that they postpone their trip! Should they do so, or go to New York anyhow? At first, Mr. Hollister thought it best for them to wait until Mr. Davis had finished his work on the Soaring Satellite.

"But Dad," Pete suggested, "he said he wanted your advice. Perhaps you can help him with his invention."

"Besides," Pam pleaded, "we ought to solve the mystery in Chinatown."

"Right," Ricky piped up. "Good detectives never wait. The clues might—might vanish."

Mr. Hollister smiled and looked at his wife. "What do you say, Elaine?"

Mrs. Hollister did not hesitate. "I have a hunch Mr. Davis will perfect his Soaring Satellite if you talk over his problem with him. The children have never been sightseeing in New York. Perhaps we should go right away."

"Hurray for Mother!" Holly exclaimed, jumping up and down with excitement.

Pete grinned. "That makes it six votes to one, Dad."

Mr. Hollister clapped an arm around Pete's shoulder. "I'll make it unanimous!" he said.

Next day the family was busy with last-minute details in preparation for their flight. Tinker, an elderly man, and Indy Rhodes, an Indian from the Southwest, both of whom worked at *The Trading Post*, promised to take good care of the business and the Hollister home. They assured the children that one or the other would visit the house daily and feed Zip, Whitenose, and the five kittens.

When all the suitcases were packed in the station wagon, Indy drove the family to Shoreham airport. They waved good-by and boarded a large four-motored aircraft.

"I guess we're the flyingest family in Shoreham," Sue said as the airliner took off. She was thinking of several exciting plane rides the family had taken previously.

The little girl sat still for some time, then got up to wander down the aisle. Reaching the lounge, she spotted a Chinese man seated in the very rear of the plane. Sue returned quickly and relayed the news to Pete and Pam.

"Maybe he's from Chinatown and knows people there," Pam said. "Let's speak to him."

After asking their mother's permission and the hostess's to speak to the Chinese, Pete and Pam walked to the lounge. The man, slender and studious-looking, was reading a Chinese newspaper. When he looked up, Pete asked politely if he would mind talking to them for a few minutes.

"I should be happy to," he said, and the Hollisters introduced themselves.

"Are you from New York?" Pam inquired.

"Yes, I am," replied the man, who gave his name as Mr. Moy.

Questioned as to whether he knew many people in New York's Chinatown, Mr. Moy smiled. "I should," he said, "I am the principal of the Chinese school there."

"Really!" Pam said, as she and her brother seated themselves on either side of Mr. Moy. "Will you tell us something about your school?"

The Chinese was pleased to do this. Laying his paper aside, he told Pete and Pam that children in New York's Chinatown go to two schools.

"They spend the day in the regular public school," he explained. "Then in the evening from five to seven, they attend Chinese school." Mr. Moy added that classes ran from the first to the sixth grade. By the time the children had completed the course, they could speak, read, and write 3,500 characters in Cantonese.

"We'd like to visit your school while we are in New York," Pete said.

"We should be happy to have you," Mr. Moy replied. Then Pam asked whether the principal knew a person named Hong Yee.

Mr. Moy was thoughtful for a few moments. Finally he said, "No, I do not know anyone by that name."

"If you should meet him, will you please let us know his address?" Pam asked. "We'll be at the Cosmo Hotel."

"I shall be glad to," Mr. Moy answered.

Pete and Pam returned to their seats, where the stewardesses served them a tasty supper. As the travelers arrived over New York, they could see below them the twinkling lights of the tall buildings and crisscross of streets.

"It looks like fairyland!" Pam remarked.

"See that big searchlight!" Ricky peered out the window beside him.

His father said the light was on top of the Empire State Building.

"Just think, we'll be going there soon!" Pam said.

The plane glided lower and the passengers fastened their seat belts. Moments later the giant airplane set down on the runway some miles outside the city and taxied to the front of the airport building.

On the ground once again, Mr. Hollister said, "And now I have a surprise for all of you. Instead of taking the bus into the city, we're going to travel the rest of the way by helicopter."

"But where will we land?" Ricky asked.

"At the heliport on the Hudson River."

"Yikes!" Ricky cried. "Let's go!"

A strong wind whistled about the Hollisters' ears and blew into their faces as they climbed into the large helicopter. There were several other passengers.

The ground crewman waved his flashlight and the helicopter taxied out onto the runway. It lifted abruptly into the air, then headed toward the tall buildings and bright lights of the Skyscraper City.

Sue leaned close to her father and spoke over the

roar of the rotor blades. "It's just as if a big skyhook pulled us up!"

Once the helicopter had gained altitude, the passengers could feel the force of the gusty wind. The craft dipped up and down, giving Pam the sensation of being on a roller coaster. She secretly hoped they would arrive at the heliport soon.

"Look! There's Times Square!" Mrs. Hollister pointed below to the display signs and the ribbony lines of automobile headlights.

"We're approaching the New York heliport," the pilot announced over the intercom. "Please fasten your seat belts."

Just then a gust of wind lifted the helicopter high into the air again. This was followed by a series of jerky motions. Suddenly the flat roof of a building appeared directly beneath them. The helicopter landed on it with a bump. The rotors whirled to a stop.

Pete expected an attendant to open the door of the aircraft, but none did. Instead, the pilot came down from the nose of the copter.

He tugged his peaked cap from his head and ran the back of his hand over his brow. "Don't worry, everything is all right," he said. "We could not make a landing at the heliport. The wind picked us up and instead we landed on a roof. I've radioed for help and it should be here soon."

At first all the passengers were quiet. When they realized, however, that they had just missed having an accident, everyone started to talk excitedly.

"You're on top of the Hotel Cosmo."

"Wait'll the kids back home hear about this!" Ricky said proudly.

As he spoke, someone put a ladder against the door of the helicopter and opened it.

"Look!" Sue squealed. "It's a fireman!"

"Right." The fireman grinned. "Everybody keep calm and watch your step on the ladder."

"Where are we, Mr. Fireman?" Sue asked, as she climbed down with the assistance of another uniformed fireman.

"On top of the Hotel Cosmo."

"Crickets!" Pete exclaimed. "That's our hotel!"

"Then you won't have far to go," the fireman said, smiling, and helped Mrs. Hollister to the pebbly roof of the tall building.

After the passengers had been ushered down through a door in the roof to an elevator on the top floor, they were met by two reporters. Both were young men with hats tilted back on their heads and pencils and pads ready for the news.

"And what is your name?" one of them asked Sue.

"We're the Happy Hollisters from Shoreham."

"Yes," Mrs. Hollister put in, "we're very happy now to have landed safely."

Once downstairs in the lobby, Mr. Hollister registered, and a bellman was sent to get the baggage from the helicopter. It was decided the aircraft should stay there until morning. When the winds quieted down, it would take off again for the heliport.

The Hollisters were shown to a suite of rooms. The girls were on one side of their parents, the boys on the other. The children went to bed at once and slept soundly.

When Mrs. Hollister called them all together for breakfast in her room, she was holding a newspaper in one hand and her eyes sparkled with excitement. "You're in the headlines, darlings," she told them.

Beneath a picture of the stranded helicopter was a story of the near accident. It gave the passenger list, including the Hollisters. Everyone except Pam was pleased to see it.

"This worries me," she said, shaking her head.

"Why, dear?"

"If Hong Yee has returned to New York, he may read this and learn that we're here."

"Don't worry. He won't hurt us," Ricky spoke up bravely.

"But he might try to stop our detective work," Pam continued.

The telephone rang and Mr. Hollister answered it. The children heard him say, "Yes," and then in a few seconds hang up.

"Who was it, John?" Mrs. Hollister asked.

"I don't know, Elaine. Somebody asked if we were the Hollisters from Shoreham. I said 'Yes.' Then the person hung up."

"Oh, dear," Pam said. "Maybe that was Hong Yee checking on us."

Her father smiled. "If it was, he's going to have a hard time locating us in the city today. We'll be moving around a lot. Our first stop is the Empire State Building to visit Mr. Davis."

After breakfast two taxis transported the family to the world's tallest building, located on Fifth Avenue between Thirty-fourth and Thirty-third streets. For a moment Ricky stood on the sidewalk, gaping at the television mast, 1,472 feet above him.

"That's really scraping the sky," he said with a whistle.

Mr. and Mrs. Hollister guided the children inside the building. An elevator took them to the sixtieth floor so fast that Sue exclaimed, "Mommy, I have butterflies in my stomach. I can feel them!"

The elevator operator grinned as the car stopped and they got out. Down the hall was an office, bearing the name *Charles Davis, Toy Designer* on the door. As they stepped inside, they saw Mr. Davis speaking with his secretary.

"Well, this is a surprise!" he said, striding over and shaking hands with Mr. Hollister. "John, I'm certainly glad you decided to come anyway. I believe you can help me work the bugs out of this invention."

"Bugs?" Sue asked, cocking her head and frowning.

Mr. Davis laughed and explained, "That means working the kinks out of an invention."

"Do kings ride in the rocket?" Sue said, puzzled.

"Kinks, not kings," Pam spoke up. "Mr. Davis wants Daddy to help him perfect the Soaring Satellite."

"I will if I can, Charlie," Mr. Hollister said. "But what you probably need is an electronics genius, which I'm not."

Mr. Davis was about to talk business with Mr. Hollister when he noticed that the children had lost interest and were looking out the windows. "Have you been to the top of the building yet?" the inventor asked.

"No," Pam replied. "We can hardly wait."

"I'll go with you," Mr. Davis offered. "But first, I want you to read this booklet about the Empire State Building. It'll help you to understand the things you see."

He handed Pam a picture pamphlet, which she read to her brothers and sisters. In a few minutes the Happy Hollisters learned that the Empire State Building, 102 stories high, is called the Eighth Wonder of the World. The building, weighing 360,000 tons, has seventy-five elevators which can travel up eighty floors in sixty seconds. There are 1,860 steps and sixty miles of water pipes in the structure.

"And contrary to rumors," Mr. Davis said when Pam had finished, "The building doesn't sway. The top moves only one-quarter of an inch."

"Oh, good," Holly said, tugging at a pigtail. "Then it's perfectly safe."

"I'll show you it is," Mr. Davis said. "Follow me." He led the family to an elevator and they soon reached the top of the building. "Here's the observatory," their host said.

"Yikes! It's big!" was Ricky's first comment. They went outside and looked about in awe at the iron fenced parapet surrounding the tower on all four sides, and at the distant scenes beyond. The wind, still lingering from the night before, tousled the hair of the youngsters as they scampered about for a view of Skyscraper City.

Looking first to the north, they saw Radio City, Fifth Avenue, and the greenery of Central Park. Eastward loomed a broad, flat-looking building which Holly said resembled a box of honey.

"That's the United Nations Building," Mr. Davis told them.

To the south was a clump of skyscrapers on the tip end of Manhattan Island. Mr. Davis said this was the famous Wall Street area.

Ricky's keen eyes roved over the harbor. "I see the Statue of Liberty!" he shouted. "I saw it first!"

"And look at those ocean liners!" Pete exclaimed as he took in the view to the westward.

Along the Hudson River many piers stretched into the water like tapering fingers. Alongside the piers were ships of all sizes, including the largest ones in the world, their white stacks glistening in the sun.

"Oh, there's so much to see!" Pam cried, trying to look in all directions at once.

"Yes, and I suggest that we grownups each take a couple of children," Mrs. Hollister said, "so they won't become lost in the crowds of sightseers."

"Good idea," Mr. Davis agreed. "There are 50,000 visitors a day to the Empire State Building, and I'd hate to see any of the young Hollisters joining Smith or Brown groups."

Giggling, Sue and Holly held their mother's hands tightly and pulled her around the observation tower again. Ricky stayed close to his father, especially when he looked over the side and down to the street below.

Pete and Pam walked about with Mr. Davis. "How are you making out with your Chinese puzzle?" he asked them.

"It's more of a puzzle than ever," Pete admitted, and told about the mysterious writing.

"I have the letter in my pocket," Pam said. "Maybe you'd like to look at it."

She pulled out the note and unfolded it. As Pam was about to hand the paper to Mr. Davis, a gust of wind blew it from her hand and took it over the side of the parapet.

"Oh!" Pam cried out in dismay.

The note drifted in the air, then, spinning round and round, dropped to the teeming street 102 stories below!

CHAPTER 8

A FUNNY MISTAKE

The Chinese note fluttered down from the top of the Empire State, finally disappearing in a canyon of buildings below.

"What if the mysterious message should fall into the wrong hands!" Pam thought frantically. "Then someone else will be looking for Yuen Foo's treasure."

When she told her fears to Mr. Davis he tried to comfort her. "Maybe nobody will find the note," he said. "It may be swept up as trash without a single person reading it."

Nevertheless Pam continued to worry about it the rest of the day. Her parents took her and the others to the Museum of Natural History to see a prehistoric dinosaur. The afternoon was spent on a conducted tour of Rockefeller Center finishing up with the show at Radio City Music Hall and dinner at one of the famous restaurants in Rockefeller Plaza. But all this failed to erase the loss of the Chinese note from Pam's mind.

Before going to bed that evening she and Pete talked about the mystery. "I think we should start to look for Yuen Foo tomorrow morning," she said.

"You mean go directly to Chinatown?"

"Yes, Pete. We ought to hurry in case someone found that note."

Mr. and Mrs. Hollister readily agreed with the

idea. "I'm going to see Mr. Davis at nine o'clock," their father told them. "Mother will accompany you to Chinatown."

After breakfast next morning Mr. Hollister announced he had a surprise for the family. He led them to the sidewalk in front of the hotel and pointed to a shiny new car parked at the curb.

"I've rented this for us," he said. "There are too many Hollisters to fit into one taxicab and I don't like the idea of using two."

"Thank you, John!" Mrs. Hollister said and kissed her husband on the cheek. Then she slid behind the wheel of the car. Mr. Hollister and Pete got in beside her while the other children sat in back.

The Empire State Building was nearby. Mr. Hollister got off there and the others continued driving south on Manhattan Island. With Pete consulting a map, Mrs. Hollister had no trouble driving to Canal Street, turning left and proceeding as far as the Bowery.

"Chinatown lies to our right," Pete said. Already shops with Oriental advertisements could be seen along Canal Street.

After making a right turn on the Bowery, Pete directed his mother to turn right again into Pell Street. Suddenly the Hollisters found themselves in the very heart of Chinatown.

"It's like entering a different world!" Pam exclaimed as she glanced about in wonderment.

Tiny shops lined both sides of the narrow street. Their colorful windows intrigued the visitors, who drove slowly past restaurants, curio shops, and Chinese grocery stores.

Pete asked his mother to stop so he could inquire about Mr. Yuen Foo. When the boy stepped out of the car the first person he met was a middle-aged Chinese man hurrying along the street.

"Pardon me, sir," Pete said. "Can you direct me to Yuen Foo?"

The man seemed startled and began to speak in broken English. Pete listened carefully as his informant gave a series of complicated directions on how to reach Mr. Foo.

The boy thanked him and returned to the car, a puzzled look on his face. "That man knows Yuen Foo," he reported, "but gave me directions for going over to the East River."

"Maybe he lives there," Mrs. Hollister remarked as she drove off.

Following Pete's directions, she took the children out of Chinatown and across the lower part of Manhattan. Soon they came to a broad boulevard running along the East River.

It was not long before they observed the massive rectangular building they had seen from the Empire State tower the day before. At its base was a line of flag poles, from the tops of which fluttered colorful pennants of the nations of the world.

Mrs. Hollister suddenly burst out laughing.

"What's the matter, Mommy?" Holly asked.

"What a funny mistake!" she exclaimed. "That man gave you directions to the U.N. Building."

"Crickets! That's right!" Pete said. "This is the United Nations. I recognize it from pictures."

"But why?" asked Sue.

"When you say Yuen and U.N., they sound alike," her mother explained, and they all chuckled about the mixup.

"Well, since we're here," Mrs. Hollister said, "let's stop in." She parked the car and led her family across a vast stone terrace in front of the visitors' entrance.

"This is fabulous!" exclaimed Pete as they stepped inside the huge building.

Pam immediately walked over to the Information Desk. She asked if any international conferences were taking place that day.

"Yes," replied the young woman behind the counter. She told them that a debate on aid to children in foreign lands was taking place in one of the chambers. She gave them all admission tickets.

The Hollisters walked down a long, wide corridor until they came to the conference room. After presenting their tickets to an usher they stepped into the balcony of a vast auditorium.

"It's something like a theater," Holly whispered to Pam.

Down in the conference hall twelve men and two women sat about a semi-circular table. Each had a microphone before him. One man was speaking a strange language.

"I think that's Russian," Mrs. Hollister said as they took their seats.

Pete was the first to discover that a set of headphones was attached to one arm of his chair. He picked them up and adjusted the set over his head, then glanced at Pam, a disbelieving look in his eyes.

"What's the matter?" his sister asked.

Pete whispered, "That man is speaking Russian but it's coming out as English."

Pam put on her earphones. She too looked surprised. "Mine's in Spanish," she said.

Hearing this, the others quickly put on their headsets and discovered that the speakers' words were being translated into five different languages: French, Spanish, English, Russian, and Chinese.

"This is done so everyone listening can understand what's going on," their mother explained.

Pete and Pam were interested in hearing what the speakers had to say about aid to children in foreign countries—sending books, teachers, even groups of American school children abroad to promote understanding and friendship. But Holly, Ricky, and Sue grew restless and wanted to move on. Finally Mrs. Hollister beckoned to them and they stepped out of the conference hall into the corridor once more.

"I understand this building has some beautiful shops downstairs," she said. "Would you like to see them?"

"Oh yes!" Holly replied and Sue added, "I'd like it if they have dolls."

Near the Information Desk the children and their mother descended a stairway to the floor below.

"This is beautiful!" Pam said eagerly as they ap-

Boingg! The noise startled the visitors.

proached a series of shops filled with merchandise from countries around the world.

Sue, Holly and Pam were intrigued with dolls of all nations while ivory elephant carvings from India fascinated Ricky and Pete.

Finally little Sue turned away from the array of dolls. She had seen something more interesting. Among the articles displayed from India was a large bronze gong hanging on the wall. Beside it was a heavy drum stick with a leather knob at one end.

Sue made her way to it. She picked up the drumstick.

"If I give it a little tiny hit," she said to herself, "I wonder what kind of noise it will make."

At first Sue gave the gong a gentle tap. A low hum was the only result. Next she stepped back and swung the drumstick.

BOINGGGG!

The loud noise startled all the visitors in the shop and one woman standing nearby nearly dropped a Grecian vase she was examining.

The sound echoed and re-echoed as Mrs. Hollister hastened over to her small daughter.

"Sue!" she cried out. "What are you doing?"

Several onlookers smiled as Mrs. Hollister took Sue by the hand and led her away from the Indian gong. As she did, a pretty Chinese woman, wearing an Oriental slit skirt, approached the family. "Your little girl did no harm," she said in a soft voice. "Please do not scold her."

"I don't like my children to cause a disturbance," Mrs. Hollister said.

"I think they are most well-behaved." the Chinese woman smiled. After introducing herself as Mrs. Tai, an employee of the U.N. shop, she said she had been noticing the young visitors from Shoreham. "It is pleasant to see a large family enjoying their trip to New York," Mrs. Tai added as she patted Sue's head.

Pete could not resist telling Mrs. Tai about the funny mistake which had brought them to the U.N. building.

"My goodness, a mixup of words," Mrs. Tai remarked. Then she added, "Perhaps my husband can help you find this Yuen Foo."

"That would be great," Ricky spoke up. "Does he work in Chinatown?"

Mrs. Tai explained that her husband owned a restaurant in the Chinese section. "He knows many people there," she said. "If you stop at the *Lotus Blossom Restaurant* on Mott Street and ask for him, I'm sure he will help you."

At the name *Lotus Blossom* Pete gave a start. He exchanged glances with Pam but discreetly said nothing about the suspicious stranger and the packet of matches Pam had found in Shoreham.

After thanking Mrs. Tai, the Hollisters went up the steps and out of the building toward their car.

"The *Lotus Blossom Restaurant*," Pam said thoughtfully. "Mother, do you think we should go there?"

"If Mr. Tai can help us, yes."

"But," said Sue, "suppose we meet that dreadful Hong Yee!"

"Don't worry," Pete said. "There are enough of us to take care of him!"

Mrs. Hollister drove back to Chinatown and parked her car. After walking along Mott Street they finally came to the restaurant. As they went inside Pam and Holly glanced about fearfully for a glimpse of Hong Yee but he was not in sight.

They found Mr. Tai immediately. He was a handsome, well-dressed man with a straight nose and classic Oriental features. When they asked him about Yuen Foo, Mr. Tai said he did not know such a person but perhaps elderly Mr. Shing, an officer of the Chinese Association, might be able to help them.

Mr. Tai directed his visitors to the Association headquarters half a block down the street. It was on the second floor of an old building laced with wrought-iron balconies on the second and third floors.

"But before you go," Mr. Tai added politely, "won't you be my guests at a Cantonese luncheon?"

Ricky whispered to his mother, "I'm hungry!"

"Me too!" Holly said under her breath.

Mrs. Hollister demurred at first but finally accepted Mr. Tai's gracious offer. Soon the family was seated around a table in his restaurant. The meal consisted of crisp egg rolls filled with chopped vegetables and bits of pork. This was followed by a steaming platter of chicken chow mein.

Luncheon over, the Hollisters thanked their host and proceeded down the street to the Chinese Association. Pete found the door and opened it, revealing dimly lighted steps leading to the second floor. Reaching the top, he knocked on another door. It was opened by an elderly man with a thin, wispy beard.

"Mr. Shing?" Pete asked.

The man nodded. "Yes, I am." Then he invited the Hollisters into a large room. In the center was a table and around the walls were rows of chairs. On the street side of the room two pairs of French doors opened onto a balcony overlooking Mott Street.

After they had introduced themselves, Pam queried Mr. Shing about Yuen Foo. The elderly man was thoughtful for a few minutes as he searched his memory.

Pete, Pam and their mother waited patiently for his reply. But Ricky, Holly and Sue wandered out onto the balcony to watch the activity in the street below.

Finally Mr. Shing smiled and nodded. "Yes," he said, "Yuen Foo lived here, in Pell Street, but he ____"

At that moment a scream from Holly interrupted Mr. Shing. Pete was the first to jump up and run to the balcony. He stepped through the French door just in time to see Ricky who was walking along the iron railing, teeter toward the street below!

"Hold on!" Pete cried and made a grab for his brother.

CHAPTER 9

THE FOO TWINS

Amid cries of fear from his sisters, Ricky fell over the railing toward the street. His arms were outstretched, fortunately, and he managed to catch hold of the railing with his left hand.

Ricky clung desperately, and just as he felt his fingers slipping, Pete's strong hands grabbed him firmly.

"Up you go," Pete said, hauling his brother to safety.

"Th-thanks," Ricky gasped, still quaking with fright.

The near accident had caused passers-by on the street below to stop and gaze up at the rescue. They clapped as soon as the young daredevil was safe again.

Pam smiled down at the upturned Chinese faces. Suddenly she cried, "Pete! Look!"

Her brother turned his head quickly in the direction she pointed. A man was hurrying to the corner, where he turned into Pell Street.

"I'm sure that was Hong Yee!" she said.

"If it was," Pete answered, "he knows for certain now that we are in New York and looking for the missing treasure."

By this time, Mrs. Hollister had led Ricky back through the French windows and was admonishing him never to do such a foolish thing again.

"I'm sorry," he said, ashamed, and gazed down at the floor. "I promise, Mother."

Mr. Shing had been disturbed too. But instead of speaking, he offered the children and their mother a bowl of litchi nuts. Mrs. Hollister figured this was to take their minds off the fright they had had.

"These nuts are from China," the man said, smiling.

When each of the Hollisters had taken some they cracked the thin, brown shells. The children nibbled on the nut meats inside. Holly remarked that they looked like small dried prunes and even had a seed inside.

"They are sweet and delicious," Mrs. Hollister said. "Thank you very much, Mr. Shing."

"We are sorry to interrupt you," Pam said. "What were you going to say about Mr. Yuen Foo?"

The old man told them that Yuen Foo had lived in Chinatown many years before. He had returned to his home in China where he had died.

"Oh dear," said Pam, disappointed that their sleuthing trail should end so abruptly.

"We understand he had a son," Pete said.

"Yes. His name is Paul. He and his family live in an apartment on Mulberry Street facing Columbus Park," Mr. Shing went on. He gave the address.

The children were excited. Perhaps the son, Paul, knew the answer to the puzzle!

The Hollisters thanked Mr. Shing for his help and for the litchi nuts, then descended the stairs to Mott Street. After walking north a block to Bayard

Street, they turned left to Mulberry and soon came to the apartment house. Paul Foo's name was over one of the doorbells in the foyer.

Just as Pete was about to push the button, the inner door of the apartment house opened and a boy and girl stepped out. Their round faces looked freshly washed, and their jet black hair was neatly brushed.

"Chinese twins!" Holly whispered to her mother. They looked about thirteen years old.

The twins smiled and then noticed that Pete was pushing the button of the Foo apartment.

The boy stepped forward. "Pardon me," he said, "do you wish to see my father?"

"Mr. Paul Foo?" Pete asked.

"Yes. We are his children." They introduced themselves as Jim and Kathy Foo.

"We'd like to talk with your father," Mrs. Hollister said.

"He's not at home," Jim replied.

"Neither is Mother," Kathy went on. She told the Hollisters that both of their parents were at work. A neighbor took care of the twins while Mr. and Mrs. Foo were away.

Jim asked if he might know the reason for the Hollisters' visit.

"It's about your grandfather, Yuen Foo," Pam said.

"He died in China about ten years ago," Kathy remarked.

Ricky and Holly turned the rope.

"We never knew him," Jim volunteered, "but my father said he was a very fine man."

Pete, realizing immediately that the Foo twins could be trusted with the secret, told them a little about the mystery.

"Our father will certainly want to talk to you," Jim said. Then he added, "Why don't you play with us in the park for a while? Our parents will be home in an hour or so."

Mrs. Hollister thought that this would be a good idea. "If you children will excuse me, Sue and I will browse around the shop while the rest of you play together."

The Hollisters now told who they were. Then together the six children crossed the street into the park which faced their apartment house. Circled by trees, the park had swings and see-saws in large concrete play areas. Jim and Kathy met other Chinese children and introduced them to the Hollisters. One girl had a long jumping rope.

"Let's skip double Dutch," Kathy said.

This made Ricky chuckle. "Why don't you skip double Chinese?" he asked.

"Oh, there isn't any!" Kathy retorted. Then she added, "Just for that, you take one end." She handed the rope to Ricky, the other end to Holly. Criss-cross went the ropes. Kathy jumped in and skipped gaily. Pam followed her.

"Faster! Faster!" Ricky called to Holly. Their hands flew and the ropes became a blur. Up and down went Pam and Kathy as fast as they could go.

Suddenly Pam's feet became tangled in the whirling rope. She lost her balance and sat down hard on the ground.

"Oh!" Pam cried out, as Kathy helped the girl to her feet. "Ricky, you went too fast," she complained.

"Okay, Sis, I'll go slower."

When the rope skipping resumed, Pete and Jim wandered away from the group.

"I'm glad you came to Chinatown," Jim said as he and Pete sat down on a park bench.

"It's great. So different from Shoreham, too," Pete remarked.

"Tell me something about Shoreham," Jim asked, and Pete described the town, Pine Lake, and their large, rambling home.

"That sounds keen," Jim said, and added, "Say, how would you like to see my room? I have something there which might interest you."

Pete grinned. "Let's go."

The apartment house in which the Foos lived was a three-story walkup. The Foo apartment was on the third floor in the front. Jim's room had a good view.

"This is swell!" Pete said, gazing around. The walls were decorated with pennants of various colleges. On Jim's desk was a sailing ship in a bottle.

"Did you make this?" Pete asked.

Jim smiled and nodded. "My father has shown me a lot about hobbies," he said. "He's an electronics engineer."

"Does he ever invent anything?" Pete asked.

"Sometimes. Maybe I'll show you one of his inventions before you leave."

Jim now opened the bottom drawer of his bureau. "Here's the surprise I have for you," he said. He pulled out a packet of red Chinese firecrackers.

Pete's eyes popped. "Where did you get these?"

Jim explained that they had been left over from the celebration of the Chinese New Year the February before.

"We can't shoot firecrackers in New York except at our Chinese celebration," he said.

"We can't in our town either," Pete replied, "except with special permission on the Fourth of July."

Jim handed over the firecrackers. "You'll keep these until the Fourth and get special permission?" He grinned.

"Honest Injun." Then Pete chuckled. "Perhaps I should say 'Honest Chinese,' " and Jim laughed.

Pete put the firecrackers in his pocket and said, "Tell me more about your New Year's celebration. It sounds like fun."

"Lions and dragons dance in the street," Jim said.

"Not for real?"

"Oh no! One of our young men dances beneath a grotesque lion's head made of silk and sticks. Other boys dance about under the long dragon's body."

"What about the firecrackers?" Pete asked.

Jim said they were used to drive the dragon and the lions off. "We throw them under their feet," he said.

"Quite a noise, I'll bet!"

"It sure is! People come from all over to watch our parades."

Jim said that "lucky money" contained in red envelopes was offered by the natives of Chinatown to the lions and dragons to appease them. He added that before their New Year's day, the Chinese always paid any debts they owed. "Our years have names, not just numbers," Jim went on.

"And what year is this?" Pete asked.

"The Year of the Dog," Jim replied, grinning. "It sounds strange to you, doesn't it? But each of our years is represented by some animal." The boy pulled a pamphlet from his dresser drawer and showed it to Pete. "Here, find out what year you were born in," he said.

Pete looked at the strange calendar. Then finding the year in which he was born, he laughed. "I was born in the Year of the Niu—the Ox." Then he added, "Let's see about my brother and sisters." Pete discovered that Sue had been born in the Year of Hu, the tiger; Holly, Lung, the dragon; Pam, Ma, the horse; and Ricky, Hou, the monkey.

"That makes sense," he said and told Jim about Ricky's near-accident a few hours before. Then he added, "Say, I know a fellow named Joey Brill back home. Let's see what his year is."

His finger followed down the calendar and came to rest on Shu, the rat. Pete grinned. "Oh well," he said, "we can't all be lucky."

He handed the calendar back. Then Jim said,

"Would you like to see my father's workroom? It's full of electrical gadgets."

When Pete replied yes, Jim led him into what appeared to be a large closet leading from the hallway of the apartment. The room, without windows, had workbenches built around two sides. On the walls above them were dials and knobs and on the benches stood all sorts of electrical equipment.

"Wow! This looks like a laboratory!" Pete said.

If Pete had been watching Jim at the moment, he would have seen a twinkle come to the boy's eyes. "Pete," said Jim, "do me a favor and touch that button." He pointed.

Pete did as instructed. What happened made him jump with alarm. The door slid shut behind him, the lights went out and a deep voice boomed out, "Surrender! You are trapped!"

CHAPTER 10

STUCK!

"Jim! Jim!" Pete called as he groped around. Finally his hands found the Chinese boy and the lights switched on to reveal Pete's new friend grinning broadly.

"Sorry to frighten you, Pete," he said. "But I just couldn't resist it."

"Resist what?"

"My father's new secret electronic invention." He explained that his father had rigged up a burglar trap in case somebody should come prowling around his work shop.

"The joke's on me," Pete said goodnaturedly. "Your dad must be a whiz." Suddenly he had an idea. "Crickets!" he exclaimed as he snapped his fingers. "This might work out fine."

Now it was Jim's turn to be perplexed. "What do you mean by that?"

Pete told him about the Soaring Satellite and that an electronics expert was needed to help perfect it.

"My father may be able to help you," Jim said as the boys left the workshop and went downstairs to the park again.

Just then Mrs. Hollister came back with Sue. "I think we'd better leave now," she said.

Jim glanced at his wristwatch. "Sorry my parents are late today. If you can't stay any longer, perhaps you can meet them another time."

"Yes," Sue spoke up. "I want to come to China-town some more. It has upstairs restaurants and downstairs restaurants and in between ones too."

The others laughed. Just then Kathy, Holly and Pam ran up.

"Chinatown must be a fascinating place to live," remarked Mrs. Hollister.

"It is fun," Jim replied. "But the area is getting crowded. Some Chinese are moving to Long Island and other places."

"I have an idea," Mrs. Hollister said. "Suppose you and your parents come to see us tonight at our hotel."

"I think they will be happy to," Kathy said. "We'll tell them."

The Hollisters said good-by and drove back to the Cosmo Hotel. Mr. Hollister was already there. He said he had worked with Mr. Davis all day on the invention, but still the satellite would not soar properly.

"Perhaps Mr. Foo will be able to help you." Pete said and told about the electronics engineer.

The family was just finishing dinner when Mrs. Hollister was summoned from the dining room for a telephone call. She returned a moment later smiling. "That was Mrs. Foo," she said. "They have accepted our invitation and will arrive at eight o'clock."

Dinner over, the family made their way to a self service elevator in the lobby. When they were all inside, Mr. Hollister shut the gate.

"Please may I push the button?" Sue asked.

Mr. Hollister lifted his daughter. Sue pressed the button for the twelfth floor and up they went.

"I think it best," said her father, "to entertain the Foos upstairs. You children can play in your rooms while we grownups talk about the satellite toy."

Promptly at eight o'clock the door buzzer announced the arrival of the Foos. Mr. Foo, a man in in his middle thirties, was slight of build and wore glasses. He shook hands with Mr. Hollister. His wife had a sweet, heart-shaped face and when she smiled a dimple showed in her left cheek.

"We are so happy to meet you," Mrs. Hollister said, as the callers walked in.

When the Foos were seated comfortably, Pam told about the book on tunnels and the Chinese note in it addressed to Yuen Foo's son.

Paul Foo was amazed. "The letter was for me!" he said. "I am the only son. But my father never told me about a hidden treasure. The part telling of a bird is especially puzzling." The man said he had received a few books from his father's estate but had not looked in them. "I lent the one on tunnels to a friend who lost it."

"And now I've lost the note," Pam said with a sigh.

Pete asked, "Did you have a statue of the goddess in your home?"

"Not while I lived at home," he replied. "I spent several years in Honolulu. It was there that I met my wife. In the meantime my father went to China where he died. His estate was settled and every-

99

thing sold by a lawyer in New York before I moved back here."

"Do you know who your father's enemies were?" Pam asked. "Was one named Hong Yee?"

Mr. Foo said he was not aware that his father had feared enemies. "I vaguely recall some trouble," he said, "but my venerable father was a very secretive man and never revealed what it was." Paul Foo told them that while in China, the elderly man had sent a cryptic message to him in Honolulu.

"It probably meant I should find the note which you did," Paul Foo went on. "The message was, *'The greatest treasure is to be found in your home.'*"

Mrs. Foo smiled. "We naturally thought this meant our children, because the twins at that time were just a year old."

"Jim and Kathy certainly are treasures," Mrs. Hollister said, smiling.

"But the information which you Hollisters have uncovered," Mr. Foo continued, "leads me to believe that my father had something else in mind when he sent that message. The English word 'help' followed out a game my father and I played when I was a boy. It meant, " 'Look for invisible writing.' ""

"It all fits together," said Pam.

Pete suggested that perhaps some old letters of Yuen Foo's would give a new clue to the mystery.

"Yes, yes," Mr. Foo said. "I have a few in my office downtown and will examine them."

He then changed the subject. Politely he asked about Shoreham and appeared very interested in Mr.

The elevator was stuck!

Hollister's description of *The Trading Post*. As this conversation was not particularly exciting to the children, they went into the other rooms to talk. No one noticed when Holly and Sue slipped out into the corridor. Their absence was noted when Mrs. Hollister started to serve ginger ale and cookies.

"Where did those two go?" she asked.

Just then the door buzzer sounded. Mr. Hollister answered. The hotel manager, a stout man, stood framed in the doorway.

"Mr. Hollister," he said, "I thought I ought to tell you that your two young daughters are stuck."

"Stuck? Where?"

"In the self-service elevator."

"Oh goodness!" Mrs. Hollister spoke up.

"We've sent for our maintenance man," said the manager. "But he won't be here for a little while."

Mr. and Mrs. Hollister excused themselves and hurried down the corridor. The elevator indicator showed that the lift was stopped between the sixth and seventh floors.

"I think I know the cause," Mr. Hollister said.

He rushed down the stairway, with the children's mother at his heels. Arriving out of breath at the sixth floor, Mr. Hollister put his mouth close to the elevator door.

"Holly! Sue!" he called.

"Yes, Daddy," Holly's voice came tearfully.

"What happened?"

"We were playing. But it isn't fun any more."

"I want to get out!" wailed Sue.

"You soon will be," her father said. "Now listen carefully."

He told them to examine the gate. Chances were it had jarred slightly open between floors. This had stopped the elevator. "If it's open, close it."

"I see it!" Holly exclaimed.

Just then there was a click and a hum. The elevator came to the sixth floor, and the door opened. The two girls rushed out and Mrs. Hollister grabbed them in her arms.

"I hope that will be a lesson to you," the hotel manager said sternly. "You should not play in elevators." He turned on his heel and left before the girls could say they were sorry.

The Hollisters stepped into the elevator and went to the twelfth floor. A cool, sparkling drink of ginger ale in ice-clinking glasses soon made Holly and Sue forget their frightening experience.

Presently Mr. Hollister said, "Mr. Foo, my son Pete tells me you're an electronics engineer."

Their guest smiled and nodded.

"I wonder if you could help me and a friend with a project," Mr. Hollister went on, and told the Chinese engineer of the trouble he and Mr. Davis were having. "We can get the satellite up to the toy balloon," Mr. Hollister went on, "but it zigzags in its orbit. Do you suppose you could help us straighten it out?"

"I'll do my best," Mr. Foo said.

Mr. Hollister gave him Mr. Davis's business card, and the Chinese said he would call on the toy inventor the following day.

When the Foo family were saying good night a little later, the Chinese woman turned to Mrs. Hollister. "I have an idea," she said. "If you want to solve a Chinatown mystery, perhaps you should live down there."

Pete overheard the remark. "You mean stay in Chinatown, Mrs. Foo? But where? I didn't see any hotels."

Mrs. Foo said that her brother and his family, who lived in the apartment across the hall from theirs, had gone to Hong Kong on a business trip.

"Their apartment is empty, and I am sure they would like you to stay there while in New York," she said.

"Oh, but we couldn't impose on such generous hospitality!" Mrs. Hollister objected.

Pete held his breath. This would be wonderful! Oh, if his mother would only accept!

Mr. Foo said, "We would be delighted to have you as neighbors for a few days."

"We would be, too, wouldn't we, Kathy?" Jim spoke up. "We like the Happy Hollisters."

The warmth of the Foos' invitation persuaded Mr. and Mrs. Hollister. After a silent, eye-to-eye consultation the children's parents smiled broadly.

"Thank you. We'll accept," Mrs. Hollister said.

Mrs. Foo reached into her handbag and gave Mrs. Hollister the key to the apartment. "Please move in tomorrow morning," she said sweetly.

After the Foos had left, Pam said, "Did you ever

see such wonderful people, Mother!" Ricky, Sue, and Holly were dancing a jig of joy.

Mrs. Hollister agreed that the Foos were among the kindest and the most unusual friends they had ever met.

Everyone bustled about next morning getting their clothes packed for the move. After Mr. Hollister had checked out of the hotel, a porter put the suitcases into their rented car, and they drove quickly to Chinatown. Kathy and Jim were waiting at the sidewalk to meet them, and helped carry the luggage to the apartment directly next door to theirs.

Mrs. Hollister gasped in delight when she opened the door. The place was furnished luxuriously with ornate furniture, deep piled rugs, beautiful vases and paintings.

"We knew you would like it," Kathy said, noting the family's pleased expressions. "We will now leave you so you can unpack." The Chinese twins bowed and excused themselves.

Mrs. Hollister selected the bedrooms for the children. They unpacked their suitcases, then walked into the living room. Just then there was a sharp rap on the door. Pete opened it. He was startled to see a tall stern-looking policeman standing there.

CHAPTER 11

A NARROW ESCAPE

"Your name is Hollister?" the policeman asked Pete.
"Yes, sir."

Ricky had rushed to the apartment door. Now he
said, "We're not burglars. Really we're not. Mrs. Foo
said our family could stay here."

The policeman smiled. "I know that." He stepped
inside. "I don't question your right to be here."

Holly hurried to call her parents. When Mr. and
Mrs. Hollister came forward, the policeman said his
name was Hobbs. "I'm here to deliver a message
from policeman Calvin Newberry in Shoreham. He
got your address from the *Trading Post.*"

"Officer Cal!" Sue cried out. "He's our friend!"

"Every policeman is your friend, little girl," the
New York bluecoat said, smiling down at Sue.

Officer Hobbs explained that Cal had phoned the
New York police and asked them to help the Hollisters solve a mystery if the children could not do it
alone. Hobbs smiled. "Cal said you probably would
not need us, though. You're good young detectives."

" 'Specially my brothers and sisters," Sue spoke
up, and the others laughed.

"I have a note for you," the policeman went on.
"It was dictated over the phone by Cal." Officer
Hobbs pulled a letter from his pocket and handed it
to Pete. The other children pressed close to him as
he silently read the message.

"What does it say?" Holly asked.

Pete replied, "Officer Cal sends his greetings. He has learned that Hong Yee has never been in trouble with the police. He seems to be all right."

"Then why did he act so strangely in Shoreham?" Pam asked.

"Cal says he's a collector of old items. Maybe that's the answer."

"It certainly is a mixed-up mystery." Holly sighed.

"I hope you can solve it," the policeman said. He told them that his beat was the Chinatown section. "If you need any help, call on me. Well, good-by now."

After the policeman had gone, the children talked about the mystery and what they should do next to solve it.

At this moment Mr. Foo and his children came to see the Hollisters. The electronics engineer asked Mr. Hollister if he would like to accompany him to Mr. Davis' office.

"I have free time this morning," he said, "and I am most eager to see the new satellite toy."

Mr. Hollister accepted the invitation and the two men went off together.

Jim now handed a small newspaper to Mrs. Hollister. "This is our Greenwich Village paper," the boy said. "That's what people in this whole section of the city read for local news."

Kathy added, "We're proud of being different down here from the rest of New York. Mother thought you might like to see our paper."

"Yes, thank you, I would," Mrs. Hollister said, and sat down to scan the articles and advertisements.

While the children made plans for their sleuthing, Mrs. Hollister suddenly exclaimed, "I think I've found a clue for you!"

"Really?" Pam said, hurrying over to her mother's side. "What is it?"

Mrs. Hollister pointed to the Lost and Found column in the classified section of the newspaper. One of the small ads read:

CHINESE NOTE FOUND NEAR EMPIRE STATE BUILD-ING. IF IMPORTANT, SEE MRS. MEEKER AT THE ADDRESS BELOW. NO PHONE.

The number given was on Canal Street, not far from the Chinatown section.

"What luck!" Pam said excitedly. "If that's the Chinese message I lost, it didn't fall into the wrong people's hands after all!"

"Let's go there right away," Pete suggested. "Will you show us the way, Jim and Kathy?"

"Of course," Jim said.

Pam tore out the clipping and together Mrs. Hollister and the children left the apartment. They hurried down to Mulberry Street and turned left onto Canal.

"It is not far from here," Jim said.

"The houses are very old in this section, aren't they?" Holly asked.

The little group stepped along briskly for a few minutes. Finally Jim led the way across the street at a green light and halted in front of a weather-beaten old tenement. Just then Sue tripped and tumbled. She hit her nose and began to wail. Mrs. Hollister stopped to brush off the dirt and comfort the little girl.

Meanwhile the other children had gone inside the building. "Oo, this place is spooky," Holly said, as they stepped into the dimly lit hallway. The place had the smell of crumbling plaster and old wood.

Pete glanced at the mailboxes, finally finding the name of Mrs. Meeker. "Can you make out whether this says the third or the fourth floor, Pam?" he asked his sister. The number, written in pencil, was very indistinct.

"I think it says the third floor," Pam replied.

"Let's go up," Ricky urged, and the four children turned the large bronze doorknob. Opening the inside door, they saw a flight of well-worn steps.

The interior of the place was cool and gloomy, and as they climbed up two flights, Pam wondered whether they should wait for Mrs. Hollister. But they went on. The third flight was even creakier than the other two.

"Well, I guess this is the apartment," Pete said, approaching a doorway at the end of a short hall. He knocked. The only answer was a scratching sound from the other side.

"What was that?" Kathy asked.

"A cat or a dog," Jim said. Pete knocked again. This time there was a low growl, and a sniffing sound.

"Hello!" Pete called out. "Are you at home, Mrs. Meeker?"

There was no reply. Instead, the growling and scratching sounds became louder. At the same time the doorknob rattled and turned slightly.

"Oh!" Holly cried, clutching Pam's arm.

"I'll bet the dog is trying to open the door and chase us," Pete said. He backed away.

The door opened a crack and a black mongrel poked his head out. He growled fiercely.

"Run!" Pete shouted, just as the dog leaped out at them.

The children dashed pellmell along the hall and down the flight of steps. Pete, in the rear, felt the dog nip his trouser leg, then heard the animal stop with a jerk.

The boy turned to look. The animal was on the end of a long chain. He had suddenly come to the end of his leash.

"Wait!" Pete called to the others who were already halfway down to the second floor and warning Mrs. Hollister and Sue to run. "It's all right now."

Out of the corner of his eye he saw the dog pulled back through the door by a thin old man. The sound of a key clicking told him it was safe for them to proceed.

"Mrs. Meeker must be on the fourth floor," Pete said, and they climbed the next flight of steps.

This time Pete's knock brought a prompt response. The door was opened by a plump, middle-aged woman with frizzy hair.

"Oh, goodness!" Mrs. Meeker exclaimed. "A whole delegation to visit me! Come in, come in."

"Run!" Pete shouted.

Pete noted that the interior of the living room was in much the same condition as the outside of the old house.

"Won't you have a chair?" Mrs. Meeker said politely to Mrs. Hollister. Then she added, "Are you selling something?"

"Oh no," Pam said. "We came to ask about the note you found near the Empire State Building."

"Oh, that!" Mrs. Meeker waved her hand dramatically. "You saw the ad in the paper? Wasn't that the funniest thing? Do you know, that note fluttered right down from somewhere and landed on my hat? Here, I'll show you."

Mrs. Meeker stepped over to a closet and brought out a hat which Pete and Ricky thought looked like an oversized pancake with some flowers on it. The hat was certainly large enough to catch a fluttering note.

"And I was so surprised," Mrs. Meeker went on with gestures. "Really, I thought someone was playing a trick on me. I reached up and there was the note, and mind you written in Chinese too. You are Chinese, aren't you?" she asked Jim and Kathy.

"We're Americans of Chinese descent," Jim answered, smiling.

"Yes, yes," the woman went on. "You know the note looked as if it might be very important. Maybe someone dropped it from an airplane, I thought, so I put the ad in our Greenwich Village newspaper that the Chinese here read."

"Please, Mrs. Meeker," Pete said, growing impatient. "We think the note belongs to us. May we have it?"

"It belongs to you?" Mrs. Meeker's mouth formed a perfect circle, and her eyes widened in surprise.

"Yes," Pam said. "We found the note in our home town of Shoreham and brought it to New York. But it blew out of my hand on top of the Empire State Building."

"Dear, dear! Now what am I going to do?" the woman said. "I don't have the note any more."

"You don't have it?" Pete gasped.

"What did you do with it?" Kathy asked.

Mrs. Meeker entwined her fingers nervously. "Why—why, I gave it to that man," she said. "He told me it belonged to him."

"What man?" Jim asked.

Mrs. Meeker said that a Chinese had called on her only an hour before. "At least he looked Chinese to me," she said. "Well, not quite. Maybe half and half."

"Hong Yee!" Pete exclaimed and shook his head in discouragement.

"The man didn't tell me his name," Mrs. Meeker said. "He claimed the note belonged to him. Was it important?"

"Yes. Very," Pete said.

"Oh, dear. I'm so sorry," Mrs. Meeker apologized.

"Perhaps," Mrs. Hollister spoke up, "the note you found wasn't ours after all. Can you tell us anything about it?"

"Not much," said Mrs. Meeker. "It was all Chinese except one word. That was 'help.'"

"Then it was our note all right," Pete told her.

Mrs. Hollister stood up and said they must go. Again Mrs. Meeker expressed her regret.

"It's really not your fault," Mrs. Hollister said kindly. "Thank you very much for trying to help the children."

Hardly a word was spoken as they walked back to the apartment, until Holly said, "Even if Hong Yee got the note, maybe he'll lose it!"

"Yes, but now he knows everything that's in the note," Pam said sadly.

As they arrived at the apartment, Mr. Foo came across the hall to see them. His face was beaming. "I have a lot of good news for you!" he said. "First, I've seen the satellite toy and I believe I can help Mr. Davis. This afternoon I'll start some experiments."

"Great!" said Pete.

Mr. Foo turned to Mrs. Hollister. "Your husband asked me to tell you that he will spend the day with Mr. Davis." Then the Chinese went on, "And now for some other kind of news. I remembered once reading in some old letters of my father's about a tunnel. So I read them again."

"What did you find out?" Pete asked eagerly.

Mr. Foo's answer was not too helpful. He had found the memorandum which mentioned the existence of a secret tunnel, but it did not say where it was. "In fact," said Mr. Foo, "I do not know whether my father was referring to a tunnel he knew about in

Chinatown or only to some tunnel he had read about in the book you bought. Anyway, I thought you could use the information."

"We certainly can," said Pete.

"But how?" Ricky asked.

"By looking around here for a real tunnel," Pete replied.

"Maybe they've been filled in by now," Pam said.

Mr. Foo assured her that there were still many tunnels in New York. "The financial district is honeycombed with them. Some date back to the Civil War and are still used to connect office buildings and banks."

"Yikes!" exclaimed Ricky. "Are the tunnels full of money?"

"One vault in particular is," Mr. Foo said, smiling. "It holds six and a half billion dollars in gold!"

"Crickets!" Pete cried out.

Mr. Foo added that the money, which was in gold bars, was stored five floors underground in the Federal Reserve Building. "You ought to see it before you leave New York," he suggested.

"But first we must continue with our detective work," Pam remarked. "Will you help us, Jim and Kathy?"

"Certainly," the Chinese children agreed, and Jim added, "We love to play detective."

Pam turned to Mr. Foo. "If your father meant a real tunnel, perhaps it's located where you used to live."

The Chinese smiled. "I do not remember ever

seeing one there, but you might look anyway. The place is no longer a dwelling."

"What is it?" Pam asked.

"A shop in Pell Street." He gave them the address.

The Hollister children looked at their mother. She smiled. "You have my permission to go if Mr. Foo thinks it's all right." When he nodded, she said, "I'll prepare lunch while you're gone."

The children's eyes sparkled in anticipation, and Pete said, "Let's go, detectives!"

CHAPTER 12

A HIDDEN FIGURE

Threading their way along the crowded, narrow sidewalks, Jim and Kathy led the Hollisters single file toward Pell Street. As they turned the corner of Mott, Pam suddenly stopped short. She grasped Kathy's arm.

"What's the matter?" Pete asked. He and the others halted.

"Look! Over there!" Pam said. She nodded toward the opposite side of the street, where a short, slim, dark-haired man was looking in a shop window. "That's—that's Hong Yee!"

"Are you certain?" Jim asked.

After staring hard at the man, Pete said, "I wish he would turn his head a bit so I could make sure."

It seemed as if the man had heard Pete's request, for he turned his face slightly as he adjusted his straw hat.

"That's Hong Yee all right!" Pete said.

"But wait," Kathy protested. "I don't think he's a Chinese."

"Why do you say that?" Pete asked. "He certainly looks Chinese to me!"

"He does resemble an Oriental," Jim agreed, "but there's something about him that's phony."

"Let's take a closer look at him," Pete suggested. Together he and Jim crossed the street and sidled up to the man, who was intently looking at some carved antique figures in the window.

All at once the fellow turned and saw the two boys. When his eyes met Pete's the stranger looked startled. Instantly he sped off.

"Stop, Hong Yee!" Pete cried. "Give us our note!"

"Catch him!" Ricky shouted.

Pete and Jim needed no urging, nor did the girls. As curious bystanders turned to watch, the children raced after Hong Yee. The fellow broke into a fast trot. With so many people on the narrow sidewalks and traffic in the street, it was difficult for his pursuers to make progress.

"Stop! Stop!" Pete called out again. "Give us back our note!"

Instead, Hong Yee put on more speed. At the corner he darted into Pell Street and ran up the block. The children saw him disappear into the doorway of a building.

"Come on!" Pete commanded, his feet flying. "We have him trapped!"

They ran through the doorway and found themselves in a narrow corridor. It led out the rear of the building into a small patch of yard. In the center of it stood an ornate bird bath. Hong Yee was nowhere in sight.

"Where did he go?" Jim said, looking around cautiously.

Several rusty fire escapes led to the roofs of the buildings, but their lower rungs were nearly six feet up from the ground. "A person would have to be an acrobat to escape up one of them," Pam commented, as her eyes roved over the rooftops. "Well, Hong Yee isn't here."

"He just seems to have evaporated," Holly remarked.

Jim spoke up. "I'm convinced now that Kathy's right about the man. He's not Chinese."

"What is he, then?" Pam asked.

"I don't know," Jim said. "Maybe some other kind of Oriental."

Disappointed, the young detectives went back through the hallway. They realized they were not far from the address of Mr. Foo's old home on Pell Street.

"Here's the place," Jim announced presently.

They stopped in front of a small shop with a center entrance. Inside the two glass windows, the children could see trinkets, curios, and knick-knacks of all kinds. Over the door hung a small neon sign announcing that this was *Miss Helen's Gift Shop.*

Kathy stepped inside, and the others followed. Behind the counter stood a young, smiling Chinese woman, dressed in a blue skirt and blouse.

"Hello," she said cheerily.

"Are you the lady named Helen?" Sue asked.

"Yes, I am. May I help you?"

"We only want to look around," Jim said. "My dad used to live here."

"Oh, yes. You must be the Foo twins. Make yourselves at home." Then with a wave of her hand she added, "I have many things for visitors to buy."

The counters and shelves were filled with a variety of Chinese items. These included paper lanterns, picture puzzles, incense, a jar of fortune cookies, coolie hats, Oriental fans, and a stack of Chinese comic books.

While the eyes of the Hollisters traveled from one group of trinkets to another, Jim and Kathy glanced about the interior of the large shop.

"This must have been divided into several rooms when Father lived here," Kathy said.

"I wonder if Grandfather really had a tunnel," mused Jim.

Suddenly Ricky exclaimed, "Yikes! I'd like to buy this!" He picked up a Chinese backscratcher. It was a long bamboo stick ending in a tiny carved hand with curved fingers.

The shopkeeper smiled as Ricky said, "You know, I've had an itch all morning right in the middle of my back."

Ricky put the Chinese backscratcher over his shoulder, but before he could touch his back, the four bamboo claws hit a beautiful Chinese lantern on the high shelf behind him.

"Look out!" Jim cried.

The lantern toppled off, but Pete leaped forward and caught it in his arms as he would a football.

"Oh!" the woman called out, and frowned. "Please be careful."

"It's not damaged," Pete said. He showed the lantern to her and then placed it back on the shelf.

"Look out!" Jim cried.

"Hereafter, watch out when you scratch," Pete warned his brother.

Embarrassed, Ricky paid for the backscratcher. He went to stand near the door so he could use it without doing any damage to the shop.

Meanwhile, Pete said to Jim and Kathy in a low tone, "Do you see any sign of a tunnel?"

"No," Jim replied. "Kathy and I have been looking at the walls. They all seem solid."

"Maybe it's down through a trapdoor," Pete suggested. He called Pam aside and whispered, "How about our buying a few things while the Foos look around some more for a secret tunnel? Then Miss Helen won't be suspicious. I'll go tell them."

Pam nodded and turned to Sue. "What would you like, honey?"

"A coolie hat," Sue replied. The shopkeeper pulled one from a rack and handed it to the little girl. Sue put it on her head and fastened the elastic under her chin.

"You look cute," the woman said.

"Do I look Chinese?"

Miss Helen chuckled, and replied, "I'm afraid not, but if you eat some Chinese fortune cookies maybe you will."

Just then Pam's eyes lighted on a small Chinese doll in the case beneath the counter. "Oh, I'd love that for my collection," she said.

The shopkeeper took out the doll and gave it to Pam to examine. "An authentic Chinese costume,"

Miss Helen pointed out. "These are made in Hong Kong."

When Pam found that she had more than enough money to purchase the doll, she said she would buy it. Pete came over to the counter and picked up a small soapstone elephant.

"That's a charm," Miss Helen said.

"I'll buy it," Pete declared.

Holly picked up a Chinese fan, unfolded it and held it over her nose. Her dark eyes darted from side to side.

"You're an imp!" Pam declared.

"The imp wants this fan," Holly said. "It costs fifty cents," Holly did not have enough money, but Pam made up the difference.

"Thank you, thank you," Holly said, bowing and fanning her face rapidly. "Honorable sister is friend."

"I want some fortune cookies," Sue spoke up, "so I can look Chinese."

"Let's buy some for Mother and Daddy," Pam suggested.

"Yes, and for Mr. and Mrs. Foo," Holly added.

Miss Helen lifted a jar of cookies off the shelf, and Pam saw that they were shaped like little tri-cornered colonial hats.

"And there is a true saying inside each one," the woman told them. She filled a bag with the confections, handed them to Pam, and turned to another customer who had entered.

Pam offered each child a cooky. The children

broke them open and removed little slips of yellow paper on which the fortunes were written.

Sue was the first to pull the paper from her fortune cooky. "What does it say, Pam?" she asked.

Her sister read it. "Waste not, want not."

"Does that mean I have to eat the whole cooky?"

"That's right," Pam said, laughing.

"Then I will!" the little girl said, and began munching the cooky.

Kathy and Jim walked over. In a whisper they said they had found nothing.

"Oh dear," said Pam. "Well, Kathy, here's your fortune." She handed the Chinese girl a cooky.

"Oh, look what mine says!" Kathy cried. As the others listened, she read, "Mystery and fortune are where you stand."

"If your fortune is correct," Jim said excitedly, "it might mean the old tunnel leads right out of this room!"

"Do you suppose you are standing on a secret trap-door to the tunnel?" Pete whispered.

Kathy glanced down. There was no sign of a trap-door. "The tunnel must open from somewhere else."

For the first time Pam noticed the back wall of the shop. It was covered with a luxurious silk hanging, but behind it there appeared to be something bulky, like the figure of a person.

The rest of the fortune cookies were forgotten for the moment as Pam asked softly, "Pete, is somebody hiding behind there?"

The boy looked for a few moments. "It's not moving," he said.

In low voices the children discussed what might be hidden behind the brocade tapestry. Then Ricky said, "Why don't we just look?"

"Oh, no," Pam cautioned, putting a hand on her brother's arm. But Ricky wriggled away, ran to the back of the store, and lifted one end of the hanging. Miss Helen turned around just in time to see him.

"Stop!" she commanded. Then speaking rapidly in Chinese to Kathy and Jim, the woman shook her head vigorously.

Ricky dropped the hanging at once, frightened by the woman's angry voice.

"What's she saying?" Pete asked.

Kathy said that someone had paid a deposit for an art object which the brocade covered. "Miss Helen does not want anyone to touch it," the girl went on.

Ricky apologized, but now the Hollisters were more curious than ever to know about it.

"What kind of an art object, Miss Helen?" Pam asked.

The woman merely shook her head. "I cannot tell you."

Pete, feeling somewhat embarrassed, thought he might offset his brother's mischief by making another purchase. He picked up a Chinese comic book and said, "How would you like this, Jim and Kathy?"

"Oh, thank you," Kathy replied. "This is the latest issue. We get them every week." The comic book was a small square one on slick paper, and was printed in beautiful colors.

Pete paid for the book and Kathy picked it up from the counter. Her eyes lingered for a moment on Miss Helen's memorandum pad and she shot a quick glance at her brother. Then they all hurried out of the store.

On the sidewalk Kathy spoke excitedly. "Jim," she said, "did you see that writing on the memorandum?"

"No. Why?"

"It was written in Chinese," she said. "The name on it was Hong Yee!"

CHAPTER 13

HO-PANG-YOW

"Hong Yee!" Pete exclaimed. "I'm going back into the shop and find out about this!" The others waited outside as Pete stepped inside the gift shop.

Miss Helen looked surprised to see him again so soon.

"I have a question," Pete said.

"Yes?"

"Is Hong Yee the person who is buying that art work?" Pete pointed to the bulky figure under the silk drape hanging on the wall.

The woman looked startled at first. Then she smiled sympathetically. "I'd like to tell you who is going to buy it," she said, "but the customer asked me to keep this in confidence."

"Can't you tell me if his name is Hong Yee?"

Miss Helen shook her head. "Sorry," she said, "the person merely paid a deposit. He might change his mind if I revealed his name."

Pete looked hard at the outlines of the hidden object. Might this be the statue of Kuan Yen? If it were, Pete reasoned, the mysterious treasure probably was to be found in this very shop!

"Thank you, Miss Helen," Pete said, and returned to the sidewalk to join the others.

"What did you find out?" Pam asked eagerly.

"Nothing. She won't tell anything."

Pam looked discouraged. "I wish Ricky had taken

a better peek after all," she said dolefully. "What do we do now?"

"Forget the shop for a while and try to learn more about Chinatown tunnels. If we only knew someone who could tell——"

"I have it!" Jim said, his face lighting up. "Mr. Moy, the principal of the Chinese School, told us something about tunnels when I was a pupil there."

"Mr. Moy!" Holly exclaimed. "We know him." The Hollisters quickly told their friends about meeting the principal on the plane trip.

"But we can't see him until five o'clock," Kathy said. "That's when school starts." As the children walked back to their apartment, the Foo twins chatted about the Chinese grade school. Both had graduated from it the year before.

"The school was such fun," Kathy said.

"And very hard too," Jim added. "Kathy and I practice speaking Chinese as much as we can, so we shan't forget any of it."

The children ate Mrs. Hollister's delicious luncheon and played together for the rest of the day. Then, after an early supper, they went immediately to the Chinese school.

"We'll go directly to Mr. Moy's office," Jim said, and led them down a corridor.

Mr. Moy was seated behind a desk, deftly counting on an abacus. Looking up, he recognized the children immediately.

"The Hollisters from Shoreham," he said. "It's so

nice of you to visit me. And how are you, Kathy and Jim?"

Pete shook hands with the principal and said, "We would like to see your school, and also ask you a question about old Chinatown."

"I'll be happy to assist you if I can," Mr. Moy replied, bowing politely. He added quickly, "How would you like to visit a first-grade classroom?"

Big smiles appeared on the faces of Ricky, Holly, and Sue.

"I want to be a Chinese girl," Sue confided with a giggle.

"We'll do our best," Mr. Moy said. "Follow me."

The children went down the corridor and turned to the right. Mr. Moy opened a door and beckoned the others to follow him inside.

The Chinese children looked up. A pretty, Oriental teacher standing at the front of the room smiled. She and the principal exchanged a few words in their native language, then Mr. Moy said to the visitors, "I would like you to meet Mrs. Tan, our first-grade teacher." The woman greeted the Hollisters and said hello to Jim and Kathy.

"This tiny girl here," Mr. Moy said, touching Sue's head, "would like to be a Chinese. Can you help her?" Chuckles rippled across the classroom, as the pupils smiled at their visitors.

The teacher asked if the Hollisters would sit down with the other pupils. Mr. Moy excused himself and left the visitors as Jim and Kathy found chairs in the front of the room.

"How would our guests like to learn a few Chinese phrases?" Mrs. Tan asked.

Sue's hand shot up at once. "Please, may I know how to say, 'Chinese little girl'?"

Mrs. Tan spoke to the class. Then the Chinese boys and girls chanted, "*Yat-go-noy-seu-hi.*"

"Oh," said Sue. She had to try it many times before memorizing the words. Her brothers and sisters recited it with her and the Chinese children.

The teacher asked Holly what she would like to learn. "Oh," the little girl said, "we're such good friends with Kathy and Jim, I'd like to learn to say 'good friends' in Chinese."

Again the class said together, "*Ho-pang-yow.*"

This was easier for the Americans to learn and they said it quickly over and over.

"One more," Mrs. Tan spoke up, looking at the Hollisters.

"You take it, Pete," said Pam, and her brother asked how to say "good luck" in Chinese.

The pupils answered together, "*Ho-sai-ki.*"

The Hollisters repeated the phrase several times, until they were sure they would remember it. Then Pam arose, feeling that the visitors had taken enough of the teacher's time. She thanked Mrs. Tan.

As the Hollisters filed out, Pam called back sweetly, "Good-by. *Ho-sai-ki.*"

Jim and Kathy led the Hollisters back to the principal's office. Mr. Moy had hung on the wall a sheet of paper six feet long and a foot wide. It was filled with bright-colored pictures and Chinese characters.

The class said together, "Ho-pang-yow."

"Isn't that pretty!" Pam said. "What is it, Mr. Moy?"

"The history of China."

"You mean it?" Pete asked.

"Yes," said Mr. Moy, smiling. "The five thousand year history of China can be seen at a glance. Pictured here is one dynasty after another. A dynasty, you know, covered many, many years when one family was in power."

"What a lot of history to learn!" Pete exclaimed.

"Yikes! Five thousand years!" said Ricky. "Why, our country only won its independence in 1776."

Mr. Moy agreed that Chinese children had much to learn about the history of their ancient homeland. "And now," the principal said, "what is your question about old Chinatown?"

Pete asked whether Mr. Moy knew of any old, secret tunnels still remaining in the area.

"Remember you told us about them one time?" Kathy reminded him.

"Oh, yes," Mr. Moy said thoughtfully. "There were some secret passageways, and I think a few remain to this day, but I don't know exactly where they are."

The Hollisters, Kathy and Jim looked at one another in great disappointment.

"But wait," Mr. Moy said. "I think I know the man who can tell you about these."

"Who?" Ricky asked.

"His name is Hootnanny Gandy. He's an old sand hog."

Holly cocked her head inquiringly. "How can a man be a pig?" she asked.

The older children chuckled. They had heard about sand hogs, and Pete explained to Holly, "A sand hog is a person who digs tunnels far underground."

"Oh," Holly said, "then he's not really a——"

"Indeed not," Mr. Moy broke in. "Sand hogs are brave and skilled workers. If it weren't for them, we might not have the Lincoln and Holland Tunnels under the Hudson River, not to mention many other tubes in our great city."

Pete asked how the Hollisters could get in touch with Hootnanny Gandy.

"He is retired from business," Mr. Moy said, "but I think I still have his address." He walked over to a filing cabinet, opened the drawer, and pulled out a letter. Then he copied Hootnanny's address on a scratch pad and handed the paper to Pam. "You'll like old Hootnanny. He's quite a character."

The children thanked the Chinese principal and went home. Because the Foo twins had chores to do next morning, they were not able to accompany Pete and Pam to the old sand hog's home. It was not far from the Chinatown area, and Mrs. Hollister gave her permission for Pete and Pam to go there alone.

The brother and sister set out soon after breakfast next morning. Locating the address, they found it was a boarding house. They knocked on the door. When the landlady answered, Pete asked about Hootnanny.

"Hootnanny Gandy?" she repeated. "He doesn't live here any more."

"Do you know where he moved?" Pam questioned.

"No, but I think his nephew does." The woman said the nephew's name was also Gandy, but she did not know his first name. "He works for the Park Services, and is employed at the Statue of Liberty!"

When Pete and Pam arrived at the apartment, they told their latest clue. Mr. Hollister praised their fine sleuthing. "I can see you're not giving up on your Chinese puzzle," he said, smiling.

"Will you take us to the Statue of Liberty right away?" Ricky asked. "I want to climb up it."

"Glad to. Does everybody want to go this afternoon?"

"Yes!"

"Please!"

"Oh, Daddy, I love you!" Holly cried, flinging her arms around her father.

"How do we get over there?" Ricky asked.

"We'll go to Battery Park and take a boat to Liberty Island," Mr. Hollister said.

Battery Park, the Hollisters soon learned, was on the southern tip of Manhattan Island. From there, ferry boats plied back and forth to Liberty Island.

Soon after eating lunch, the Hollisters set out and drove downtown. After their car was parked, the children's father bought tickets for the sight-seeing boat to the Statue of Liberty.

"Here comes our boat now!" Pete exclaimed as he

noticed a long, white three-decked craft which moved in alongside the dock. The Hollisters watched, fascinated, as hundreds of people poured off the boat, making room for a long line waiting to get on.

"Miss Liberty is perhaps the best known statue in the world," Mrs. Hollister told her children as they moved along toward the gangplank. After giving their tickets to the attendant, Holly and Ricky skipped on ahead. Pete and Pam followed them, while Mr. and Mrs. Hollister brought up the rear with Sue.

The younger children immediately raced up to the top deck and leaned on the railing, gazing off to the statue, which looked small from this spot. When Mrs. Hollister caught up with them, she told the children something about the great memorial which the French had given to the American people.

A young Alsatian sculptor, Frederick Auguste Bartholdi, was sent to America to study and discuss the project. As Bartholdi entered New York harbor, he conceived the idea of a colossal statue to stand at the very gateway of a new world to represent the one thing man finds most precious, liberty.

"Why is Miss Liberty green?" Holly asked, as the engine of the sight-seeing boat throbbed and the craft headed across the great inner bay.

Mr. Hollister explained that the statue was made of copper, which turns green when left out in the weather.

Now the great statue loomed large as the boat came closer to Liberty Island. Pam's interest was divided between the statue and finding Hootnanny

Gandy's nephew. If he could reveal the whereabouts of the old sand hog, they might find a clue to the hidden treasure in Chinatown.

"This ride is great!" Pete remarked, looking back at Skyscraper City.

In a little while the boat glided alongside the wharf at Liberty Island and the passengers debarked. The island was larger than the Hollisters had imagined. To the left of the dock were some utility buildings. A new one, recently finished, still had a small cement mixer standing alongside the concrete wall. As the Hollisters walked on, they could see the island's park stretching to the right, at the tip of which the statue rose majestically into the sky.

The Hollister children dashed ahead of their parents, and entered a doorway at the base of the monument. "Hurry, Mother and Dad," Ricky called. "There's an elevator that will take us halfway up."

The family crowded into a small elevator which took them up ten stories to an observation deck. Stepping from the elevator, the children saw three uniformed Park Service men directing the sight-seers up the narrow spiral stairway to the top of the statue, twelve stories above.

"Does Mr. Gandy work here?" Pam asked them.

A stout, middle-aged man stepped forward and smiled. "I'm Henry Gandy," he said.

"Are you Hootnanny's nephew?" said Pete.

"That's right."

"Do you know where your uncle lives?" Pam questioned.

"Yes, in Greenwich Village."

When the children said they would like his address, Mr. Henry Gandy wrote it on a slip of paper and gave it to Pete.

"We want him to help us find a tunnel connected with an old Chinese mystery," Ricky explained.

"My uncle will be glad to talk about old tunnels," Henry Gandy said. He chuckled. "Once you get him started, it'll be hard to stop him!"

The children thanked the attendant. Then, with their parents, they worked their way high up the spiral staircase to the top of the statue.

"Where are we in Miss Liberty?" Holly asked, as she peered out a set of little windows that looked across the bay.

"We're right under the crown on her head," Mrs. Hollister told them.

"I can't see much except boats and boats," Holly complained.

Their mother said that they would get a much better view from the observation platform below. After making their way down the staircase, they met Mr. Gandy again.

He walked out on the observation parapet with them. The guide told them that the statue rested atop a granite pedestal built on the foundations of old Fort Wood. "This place used to be known as Bedloe's Island," he said, "but the name was changed to Liberty."

The Hollisters learned that the statue was 152 feet high and the pedestal almost 150. Sue shook her head as if this did not seem possible, then with a grin said, "She's the biggest dolly in the whole wide world."

"I guess you're right." Mr. Gandy laughed, then added, "Miss Liberty was dedicated by President Grover Cleveland on October 28, 1886."

With the wind blowing in their faces, the Hollisters looked up at Miss Liberty, then out over the magnificent Manhattan skyline. Finally they said good-by to Mr. Gandy and descended in the elevator.

"I'm hungry," Ricky announced, when they were on the ground again.

"I am too," Holly chimed in.

Mr. Hollister boyishly admitted that the long trek had given him an appetite also. "I see a little restaurant over there," he said, indicating one of the low buildings. "We'll get a snack."

As they finished, Ricky said he could eat another frankfurter, but his father shook his head. The last boat for the day to take away visitors was ready to leave. As the Hollisters hurried toward the pier, the children's father called out, "We'll go to the top deck."

As Ricky passed another attendant, he asked, "Do any visitors ever get left on the island at night?"

The man smiled. "No, sonny," he answered. "It can't possibly happen and never will. We search every inch of the island before the last boat leaves."

The crowd of visitors surged toward the gates and the Hollisters became separated as they boarded the boat. But one by one they met on the top deck until all were there but Ricky.

"Where is he?" Mrs. Hollister asked, annoyed.

"He's probably at the refreshment counter getting another frankfurter," Pete said.

"Will you go see?" Mrs. Hollister asked.

Pete descended the stairs to the middle deck, but Ricky was not at the refreshment counter. Walking around, Pete searched the boat thoroughly. But he did not find his brother.

Finally Pete went to tell the rest of the family. Mr. Hollister made inquiries of several people, including the boat's personnel. No one had seen freckle-faced, red-haired Ricky Hollister!

CHAPTER 14

THE FLICKERING FLASHLIGHT

Mrs. Hollister was alarmed. "Oh, where could Ricky have gone?" she cried out.

"He must be around here somewhere," her husband said hopefully as he glanced at the throng of passengers debarking from the sightseeing boat. "He'll show up."

But as the crowd thinned out, Ricky was still not to be seen. Every one of the Hollisters secretly feared that the boy might have fallen off the boat, but none said so aloud.

"I'll phone Liberty Island and see if he was left behind," Mr. Hollister said, and hastened to the small building where he had bought his tickets.

Pete ran alongside his father. "But the guard at the island told us nobody was ever left behind after the last boat, Dad."

"They don't know Ricky," Mr. Hollister said. "He's just imp enough to try something like that to prove a point."

By the time he had dialed the number, the rest of the family stood outside the telephone booth, anxiously waiting. The phone rang on Liberty Island and a guard answered. After a couple of minutes' conversation, the others heard Mr. Hollister say, "Thank goodness!" and a look of relief spread over his face.

"Hurray! He's all right!" Holly shouted, and danced up and down.

Mr. Hollister spoke a little longer and then hung up. He opened the door. "Well, Ricky is safe over on the island. Guess where he hid!"

Guesses ranged from the top of the Statue of Liberty to the restaurant where they had eaten.

The children's father shook his head. "No, the guards checked the likely places, but they forgot one."

"What was that? Please tell us," Holly begged.

"The cement mixer!"

"What!" Mrs. Hollister exclaimed.

"Yes, he hid in the cement mixer. The guard said he poked his head out only a few moments ago and they saw him."

"That monkey!" Mrs. Hollister cried. "How are we going to get him?"

"They have a small speedboat on the island," Mr. Hollister said. "Mr. Gandy is bringing him over in that."

The family hurried to the dock. Eagerly they looked out over the stretch of water, which reflected the slanting rays of the low-lying sun. To pass the time, Mr. Hollister bought the children ice cream cones from a vendor with a small white cart.

Minutes went by, until finally Pete sang out, "Here he comes! I see him now!"

A speedy motorboat headed their way. As it drew closer, Ricky waved from the rear seat. The boat pulled alongside the wharf. Ricky stepped out.

"Here's your son," said Mr. Gandy. "No hard

feelings, but Ricky, I'd advise you not to try such a trick again."

"I—I won't," Ricky replied, looking very repentant.

"I'm sorry this happened, Mr. Gandy," said Mr. Hollister, as the motorboat started back toward Liberty Island.

Mr. and Mrs. Hollister did not scold Ricky, who now was looking at the ice cream cones the other children were eating. But his parents did not suggest that he have one.

Ricky did not complain. As the family walked across Battery Park, though, the boy lingered behind with a crestfallen shuffle. Sue noticed a tear run down his cheek.

When Mr. and Mrs. Hollister reached the car they glanced back at their children. Ricky was not the only one in the rear. With him was Sue, forcing her brother to take a few licks of her ice cream cone. The others smiled.

In their car once again, the Hollisters quickly forgot Ricky's escapade and the talk turned to the mystery. "Meeting Henry Gandy was good, wasn't it?" Holly said.

"Yes," her mother agreed, adding that it was too late in the day to look up Hootnanny. "You can continue your sleuthing first thing in the morning."

The family returned to their apartment. While the younger children helped set the table, Mr. Hollister and Pete went to a nearby restaurant and brought back containers of Chinese food.

Pam served it expertly. Everyone enjoyed the *won ton* vegetable soup and the egg *foo young*. Holly and Sue helped their mother wash and dry the dishes while Pam examined the new doll she had bought for her collection. She was busy turning its head from side to side when suddenly she cried out, "Oh, it came off!"

"What?" Mrs. Hollister asked.

"The doll's head. Look here."

Mrs. Hollister hurried over to look at it, and said she felt sure the toy had been faulty. "I'm certain the shopkeeper will give you a new doll in place of it, Pam."

"Will you go with me, Mother, right away?"

"It's growing dark," Mrs. Hollister said. "The store may be closed."

"Let's see, anyway," Pam urged.

Mrs. Hollister smiled. She took off her apron and threw a lightweight jacket over her shoulders. "We'll go," she said.

They made their way to Pell Street. By this time the neon lights of Chinatown glowed in soft, intriguing colors. But Mrs. Hollister and Pam found that the lights in Miss Helen's sign had been turned off.

"Oh, the store's closed," Pam said, disappointed.

"Maybe she is just locking up," Mrs. Hollister suggested, and they peered through the show window.

A flashlight suddenly flickered on the silk wall covering at the rear. As the Hollisters gazed, the covering fell to the floor and the flashlight played over a Chinese statue which the silk had concealed.

Pam pressed closer for a better look. But in doing so, she accidentally pressed the glass which set off a burglar alarm inside the shop.

Instantly the flashlight clicked off. There were running footsteps. Then the door flew open and a masked man dashed from the shop.

"Oh Mother!" Pam cried out, as he nearly knocked Mrs. Hollister to the sidewalk. The stranger ran toward the Bowery and escaped around the corner.

While the Hollisters watched him, too stunned to move, other footsteps were heard running down the stairs leading from the street to quarters on the second floor. Miss Helen ran out.

Seeing the two poised in the darkness beside the open door of her shop, the woman shouted, "Help! Police! Robbers!"

An excited crowd gathered quickly, hemming in Pam and her mother, while Miss Helen again called loudly for the police. Moments later Patrolman Hobbs shouldered his way through the crowd.

"What's going on here?" he asked.

"These persons just came out of my locked store," the shopkeeper said.

"Oh, no, we didn't," Pam protested, still clutching her broken doll.

"You're mistaken," Mrs. Hollister said. "We were looking in the window when a man dashed out."

The policeman recognized the Hollisters. He said he was certain they were innocent, but added, "Tell me what happened."

"Is that the Chinese Goddess of Mercy?"

145

After Mrs. Hollister had finished her story, Patrolman Hobbs said, "Let's go inside and take a look."

Together the officer, Miss Helen, Pam and her mother entered the store. Miss Helen turned on the lights. Everything was just as the Hollisters had said. The silk hanging lay on the floor, revealing a wooden statue of a Chinese woman. The mystical-looking figure was seated on a rug-covered bench, her hands folded in her lap. Her beautiful face was slightly lowered and she wore a placid expression. The statue was poised on a solid three foot cube.

After Miss Helen had glanced about the place, she sighed. "Well, nothing appears to have been taken, thank goodness."

"I wonder what the prowler wanted," Pam remarked.

The policeman thought that perhaps he was trying to figure out how he could steal the statue.

Pam's heart thumped as she asked the next question. "Is that Kuan Yen, the Chinese Goddess of Mercy?"

The shopkeeper's eyebrows rose in surprise. "Yes, how did you know?"

"I have heard the name mentioned before," Pam said, trying to appear unconcerned.

"Not many people know——" Miss Helen started to say, when an angry voice sounded at the door.

"Release them! I demand it!"

Pam turned to see Mr. Foo entering the shop. He said to the policeman, "Mrs. Hollister and her daughter Pam are friends of mine."

"Goodness!" Mrs. Hollister exclaimed. "How did you know we were here?"

"Stories travel fast around Chinatown," Mr. Foo replied. The agitated Chinese was soon calmed by Patrolman Hobbs who said that it was obvious that Pam and her mother were not thieves.

Miss Helen apologized, saying she hoped they would consider her outcry only a natural mistake. Nothing in the shop had been disturbed, but she wished the policeman would search for the intruder.

Pam described the man who had dashed away, and added, "I think his name is Hong Yee."

"Hong Yee?" the shopkeeper asked. "He is the one who put a deposit on Kuan Yen."

"I think he did that," Pam said, "to be sure you would not sell the statue."

"But why would he be prowling around my shop?" Miss Helen went on.

Patrolman Hobbs said that many questions would be answered when the intruder was apprehended. He hurried out to search for him.

Pam turned to the Chinese proprietor and asked for further information about the statue.

"Mr. Foo no doubt knows more about it than I do," the shopowner said. "It once belonged to his father and was left in this house."

"Belonged to my father?" Mr. Foo said. "I knew nothing of this statue."

"It was well hidden," Miss Helen told him. "When I took over the shop, there was a large built-in wardrobe here, sticking out into the room. I decided to have it removed. The men found the wardrobe had a false back which completely hid the statue."

"How amazing!" said Mrs. Hollister.

Miss Helen nodded and went on, "I left the statue in the very spot where it was found, hoping a buyer would recognize its value and buy it."

"Whatever you do," Pam begged, "please don't sell it now. Please."

"Why?"

"Because it's the center of a mystery we are trying to solve," Pam replied.

Although Miss Helen seemed confused, Pam thought it best not to reveal the entire secret to her, and a slight nod from Mr. Foo indicated he approved.

After the shopkeeper had promised to do nothing more with the Kuan Yen piece until she heard from Mr. Foo, Pam told the reason for their visit, and held up the broken doll. Apologizing profusely, Miss Helen gave her another and they left.

Back at the apartment the two families had a conference, deciding what should be the next step in solving the mystery.

"Mr. Foo, if Kuan Yen is guarding the treasure, as your father said in his letter," Pam reasoned, "maybe the valuable object is concealed in some part of the statue."

"Or underneath it," Pete said.

"Maybe behind it," Jim declared, his eyes flashing with excitement.

"Let's not jump to conclusions," Mr. Hollister

warned his young sleuths. "Perhaps Hootnanny Gandy will supply the answer."

"Yes," Kathy said. "He knows all about tunnels, especially the ones in Chinatown."

"We'll find him first thing in the morning," Pete declared.

After breakfast the next day he asked if he and Ricky might hurry over at once to see the old man.

"All right," Mrs. Hollister agreed. "It's not necessary for all of us to go. But take a cab."

She gave him enough money and the boys set off. Pete hailed a taxi cruising around Columbus Park and gave Hootnanny's address in the Village.

As Ricky stepped inside and shut the door, he noticed a man with his back to them hail a cab directly behind the boys. The fellow got in, crouched low in the back seat, and pulled a black felt hat down over his forehead.

The Hollisters' cab set off. The other taxi followed close behind.

"Say, Pete," Ricky spoke up nervously, "I don't like this. I think we're being followed."

Pete relayed Ricky's suspicion to their cabbie.

"I'll shake him off," the man stated. He quickly turned down one street, then up another. But the car behind kept them in sight.

CHAPTER 15

HOOTNANNY'S HUNCH

"I see our chance!" the cab driver said suddenly. The street light at the intersection they were approaching was green but would not stay that way long. The cab scooted across just as the light turned amber, then red.

"We made it!" Pete cheered. "Good for you!"

The cab driver grinned. "Pretty nosy fellow behind me," he said.

"I'm glad we shook him," Ricky declared.

Presently they pulled up in front of a new apartment building. As the two boys alighted, the cabbie remarked, "This is one of those new, low cost housing projects. You may have heard about them."

"It's keen," Ricky said.

Hootnanny's apartment was on the street level. The brothers walked down the hall and Pete pressed the buzzer. The door was opened by a tall, gaunt man with stooped shoulders.

"Come in, come in, boys. If you're looking for old Hootnanny, the sand hog, I'm your man!"

Hootnanny Gandy, they could see, once had been a man of great physical stature. He extended a gnarled, thin hand when the boys introduced themselves, and looked at them with piercing gray eyes behind bushy brows. But oddest of all was the elderly fellow's bristly gray hair which stood up on his head like a whisk broom.

The old sand hog walked with a limp to a chair on the other side of the neat living room. He sat down and indicated chairs for the brothers. "Now, if you're thinkin' about goin' into the sand hog business," he said abruptly, "I'd advise you to try something else."

"No, we're——" Pete started to say.

"Bein' a sand hog is a very dangerous business—but interestin'," old Hootnanny continued with a wink. "You discover the funniest things under ground, like old coffins, gold coins and Indian trinkets."

"But diggin' in the mud is not worth a hootnanny," the old fellow went on, pounding a bony fist into the palm of his hand for emphasis. "I think a young boy today would rather be a sailor or maybe a steeplejack or some other safe occupation like that."

"But—but——" Ricky started to say.

"No buts about it," the old fellow spoke on, his eyes darting from one boy to the other. "Bein' a sand hog is the most dangerous job in the world and anybody who says it ain't, don't know a hootnanny from a bag of beans!"

Mr. Gandy leaned forward and shook his finger to mark his words. "Let me tell you somethin'," he said. "I was helpin' to dig a tube under the North River —that's the Hudson, you know—when my foreman punched a hole right through the roof."

"The roof of the river?" Ricky asked.

"No, the roof of the tunnel."

Pete was fascinated. "What happened?" he asked.

"Well, this foreman of mine tried to stuff straw into the hole, but when he pushed his hand up he got sucked into it himself."

Seeing that he had the boys spellbound with the story, Hootnanny set back in his chair and grinned broadly. "Well, the foreman stayed there a while, kicking his feet," Hootnanny continued. "Then all of a sudden, *whomp*, up he went!"

"Yikes!" Ricky blurted. "Where did he go?"

The old sand hog said that the pressure shot the foreman through five feet of mud, then, the water itself. "He spouted up like a blowin' whale!" Hootnanny went on, "and kept goin' twenty-five feet into the air."

"Was he hurt?" Ricky asked, his eyes the size of silver dollars.

"Awful shook up," Hootnanny said sadly, and he added, "That's when I quit bein' a sand hog."

"You didn't dig any more tunnels?" Pete asked.

"Not under rivers," the old fellow replied. "Oh, I dug plenty of tunnels after that. But mostly private ones in the city."

"That's just what we want to talk to you about, Mr. Hootnanny," Ricky said.

"Right," Pete added. "Do you remember digging a tunnel for Yuen Foo in Chinatown?"

The old fellow scratched his bushy head and thought hard. "Yuen Foo," he mused. "Can't rightly remember. You say Chinatown? I dug several tunnels there many years ago."

"Please try hard to remember," Ricky begged. "It's very important to us, Mr. Hootnanny."

The old sand hog rested his chin in his bony hand. "Hmm," he said. "Now it comes back to me a little."

"Then you did dig him a tunnel!" Pete said excitedly.

"Reckon I did, but I can't remember exactly where it was, but I have a hunch——"

Pete realized that he should not push the old man into trying too hard to remember. In that case he might forget about the old tunnel altogether. "Maybe if you come to Chinatown you might recall it," he suggested.

"Reckon I might at that," the old sand hog said. "All right, I'll come. What time?"

"Three o'clock," Pete said. "We'll meet you at the corner of Mott and Pell."

The brothers thanked the old man and left. Going out to the street again, Pete held up two crossed fingers. "Oh, I hope he remembers!" the boy said, grinning.

Again Pete hailed a taxi and this time the boys proceeded toward their apartment without being followed. But they could not forget their pursuer, or help wondering what he wanted. Both boys discussed who it might have been. Hong Yee?

"Hard to tell with his hat pulled over his face," Pete remarked.

Arriving home, he and Ricky found their sisters bubbling with excitement. "We're going to see a tunnel!" Holly declared.

"When?" said Ricky.

"Right away!"

"Where?"

Pam told her brothers that Mr. Foo had just tele-phoned, asking the Hollister children to meet him at a downtown restaurant for lunch. "Then he's going to take us to the Federal Reserve Building to see the gold."

The rest of the family was intrigued to hear about Hootnanny Gandy and eager to meet him in China-town that afternoon. Meanwhile, however, Mr. and Mrs. Hollister drove the children to the restaurant where they left them with Mr. Foo.

"Daddy and I are going shopping," Mrs. Hollister said to the youngsters. "We'll see you later."

When lunch was over, Mr. Foo led the children to a massive granite building nearby.

"Boy, it looks like a fort!" Ricky said glancing about.

Pete pulled open a heavy iron door and they entered. The first thing they saw was a uniformed guard seated behind a desk. Mr. Foo introduced him-self and the children, saying that they would like to see the gold vault.

"Step this way." The guard directed the group to another armed officer who said, "Come with me."

He led the visitors to an elevator. When they were inside, the door slid shut and down they went.

"We're going five stories underground," the guide said.

Finally the lift stopped. Now the Hollisters were

led out into a passageway guarded by steel bars from floor to ceiling. They could look beyond this into a gigantic vault.

"Oh look! See the gold!" Holly called out. "It really is yellow."

Another guard opened a door in the wall of steel bars and the party stepped through. He led them into a high-ceilinged vault full of cages.

"It looks like a zoo without animals," Ricky whispered to Pete.

Pam asked, "How many feet down are we?"

"We're fifty-five feet below sea level," the uniformed man told her. "This vault you're in holds six and a half billion dollars worth of gold."

"Billions! Crickets!" Pete exclaimed.

"In the cage directly in front of you," the guard went on, "is a hundred million dollars." He pointed to the gold bars piled one atop the other.

"How much do the bars weigh?" Pam asked.

She was told that each bar weighs about twenty-eight pounds and is worth fourteen thousand dollars.

Sue, who had been quiet up to this point, asked, "Please may I take one home to Daddy and Mommy?" Everyone laughed, including the guard, and Pete said, "Sue, we can't have this gold, but maybe Hootnanny can help us find a treasure like it."

"Let's hurry back and look for one right away," Holly remarked.

As they ascended in the elevator to the first floor, Pete glanced at his watch. "It's nearly time for us to meet Hootnanny Gandy," he told Mr. Foo, who took them home.

Mr. and Mrs. Hollister were already back. They decided that Sue should remain at the apartment for a nap while the four other Hollisters, along with Kathy and Jim, would meet Hootnanny. They found him at three o'clock sharp on the corner of Mott and Pell Streets.

"Hello, Hootnanny!" Pete said, running up to the old sand hog. "I want you to meet two of my sisters and our friends, Jim and Kathy Foo."

After shaking hands with them, Hootnanny said he had been wandering around Chinatown for the past half hour. "I'm sure I dug a tunnel up the street here," he declared.

"Pell Street?"

"Yep. And if my name's Hootnanny, I believe it was right there inside that store." He pointed to Miss Helen's Gift Shop. "Only it used to be a house."

The children's hearts thumped with excitement as they hurried along the street. It seemed as if at last the mystery might be solved!

"Oh boy, you're good detectives!" Jim said as he and Pete ushered the old sand hog into the gift shop.

Miss Helen was very kind to him and the children. She listened attentively as Pam quickly told her about what they suspected.

"A tunnel in my store?"

"Yep," Hootnanny said. "I believe it was in here.

"I believe the tunnel was inside that store."

I remember I had the dickens of a time carting the dirt out."

The old tunnel digger glanced about the place as if trying to figure out exactly where the tunnel had been. As he started to walk toward the statue of Kuan Yen someone called into the front door.

"Mr. Gandy, your nephew is outside and wants to see you."

Hootnanny looked around. "Hey, who was that?"

All eyes turned to the door. The bright sun outside framed the figure of a slender man with a peaked cap.

"Come on, Hootnanny," the man urged. "Your nephew's waiting in my cab."

The Hollisters and the Foo twins stood aside as the old sand hog walked from the store. As he reached the curb he was suddenly seized by two men who pushed him into the open door of the taxi.

One of the fellows jumped in beside Hootnanny. The door slammed shut. The other man started the car and whizzed down Pell Street!

CHAPTER 16

A LOST ROCKET

Hootnanny's departure had been so sudden that the Hollisters and their friends were stunned. The cab had disappeared by the time the children reached the sidewalk.

"That's a strange way to treat an uncle," Holly remarked. "I'm surprised at Henry Gandy."

Pam had a worried look. "I'm afraid it wasn't Hootnanny's nephew," she said uneasily.

"Who, then?" Jim asked.

"Hong Yee!" Pete exclaimed. "Is that what you think, Pam?"

His sister said yes. "I think Hong Yee took Hootnanny away to make him tell about the old tunnel."

Pete thought they should notify the police immediately. Officer Hobbs came around the corner of the Bowery and the children hurried up to him.

"Hootnanny's been taken away," Pete stated, and told what had happened.

Immediately the officer hurried to a call box nearby and telephoned the report to headquarters. Two minutes later, a police car sped to the scene and two more policemen got out. They asked each of the children to tell the story, then spoke to Miss Helen.

"It does look as if he'd been forcibly taken," one of the officers said. He stepped back into the police car and broadcast an order to other patrol cars cruising in the great city.

The description of the get-away taxi, as told by Pam, was of some help. Unfortunately, however, none of the youngsters had noted the license number.

In order to make doubly sure that it was not Henry Gandy who had whisked the old man away, the police telephoned to Liberty Island. Henry Gandy was on duty there. He told them he had not seen his uncle for several days, and was alarmed to learn of Hootnanny's sudden disappearance.

After the police had driven off, the young sleuths entered the store again. Miss Helen cooperated graciously as the search began. The children felt sure Hootnanny had indicated the tunnel was near the statue. They pounded the walls, listening for hollow spaces behind them. The partitions were solid.

"Miss Helen, may we move the statue?" Pete asked. "The opening to the tunnel may be underneath."

She nodded and the children gently pressed against the heavy base. It did not move. They pushed harder. Still the wooden block remained in place.

"It must be nailed down," Ricky guessed, and Pete said, "Crickets! We're getting no place. And just when old Hootnanny was about to show us where he had dug the tunnel!"

"I guess we'll have to wait until the police find him," Pam said with a sigh.

She thanked the shopkeeper for her help, and the six children returned home. Climbing the stairs, they heard excited voices coming from the Hollister apartment.

"Something must have happened!" Pete exclaimed. "Come on! Let's hurry!"

Entering the apartment, they found not only Mr. and Mrs. Hollister and Sue but Mr. Foo and Mr. Davis as well.

"They've done it!" Sue shouted. "It works, it really works!"

"You mean the Soaring Satellite?" Pam asked.

"Yes," Mr. Hollister said, smiling broadly. He turned to Jim and Kathy. "Your dad is responsible for perfecting the new toy."

"He's a great engineer!" said Mr. Davis, beaming. "Look here."

On a table in the center of the room lay a large balloon painted to resemble the moon. Beside it was a small toy rocket, eight inches long, poised on a launching pad. Next to this was a control box with dials and levers.

"May we see it work?" Pam asked, stepping over to look at the unusual toy.

"Of course," Mr. Davis replied.

First he released the balloon from the string which held it to the control box. It rose into the air, finally coming to rest against the ceiling.

"And now for the rocket," Mr. Davis said eagerly.

Mr. Foo seated himself in front of the control panel, as the children looked on in breathless anticipation. He pressed a button. There was a humming, hissing noise, and the toy rocket rose from the launching pad. White smoke came from the rocket tubes as the rocket rose higher and higher. Then the Chinese engineer turned a dial.

"It's going into orbit!" Pete cried out.

At first slowly, then faster and faster, the rocket whizzed around the moon.

"The Soaring Satellite's working!" Ricky cried. "Boy, this is keen!"

"I just can't believe it," Mrs. Hollister declared. "What a wonderful toy!"

"We'll sell millions of them," said Mr. Davis, his eyes alight with happiness.

What followed made the onlookers gasp in amazement. Mr. Foo slowly turned another dial. The Soaring Satellite circled lower and lower, then made a perfect landing on the launching pad.

The children clamored for a try at the new toy. Mr. Foo explained how it worked, but added, "The dials must be handled very carefully; otherwise, the Soaring Satellite will overshoot its mark."

Pete insisted that Kathy and Jim be the first to play with the new toy. The girl sat down in front of the control panel and did exactly as her father had instructed. Up went the Satellite and circled the make-believe moon. When it landed, the others cheered.

Jim was next to try his hand. He too, operated the new toy successfully. Then Pam, Pete, Holly, and Ricky, much to the delight of their parents, made the toy Satellite soar around the toy moon.

The Soaring Satellite sailed out the window.

"Please may I try?" asked Sue, when the others had finished.

Mrs. Hollister glanced toward Mr. Foo. "Let her try," he smiled, and Sue took her place before the launching pad. Her chubby fingers grasped the dials.

"Careful now," her father cautioned. "Don't work it too fast."

The little girl was shaking with excitement as she set the rocket into a perfect orbit. "I'm a space girl!" she cried out gleefully, then added, "How do I get it down?"

"Here, turn this dial," Mr. Foo directed, pointing.

Sue's fingers went to the right dial, but in her excitement she turned it too quickly.

The Satellite soared wildly around the room!

"Look out! Duck!" Mr. Hollister cried out.

Throwing their hands up to shield their heads, the onlookers crouched down. The Soaring Satellite made wider circles, coming lower and lower. Then *whiz!* it sailed out the window.

"Oh, dear!" Sue wailed. "I've broken the rocket!"

"Where did it go?" Pam asked excitedly.

"To the real moon!" Holly burst out.

Pete was first to reach the window. "There it is, circling over the park."

Now Mr. Foo had his hands on the controls, and gradually the Soaring Satellite circled lower and lower.

"Oh, oh," Jim cried out, "it's landed in a tree."

"Crickets!" Pete said. "The highest one in the park."

"I wonder if the rocket's broken," Pam worried.

"We'll soon find out," Pete answered. He raced to the door, down the steps, across the street, and into Columbus Park.

As the other children and the grownups hurried behind him, Pete called, "I'll shin up."

The nimble boy threw his arms around the tree trunk and inched his way to the first limb. Once there, he climbed quickly among the branches. As he neared the top, Pete was reminded of Joey Brill and the trick in the school playground in Shoreham.

His thoughts quickly returned to the marooned toy, sticking through the leaves above his head. Pete reached up and grasped it. A quick examination showed that the Soaring Satellite had not been damaged.

"It's okay," he called down.

"Good!" Mr. Hollister shouted. "Easy does it, son. Come down slowly."

With the Soaring Satellite in one hand, the boy descended the tree. "I guess I can jump down the rest of the way," he said, poised on the lowest limb.

"Here, toss me the Soaring Satellite first," his father ordered. Pete did so and Mr. Hollister caught the toy. "Okay. Jump."

As Pete's feet left the limb, one of his trouser pockets caught on a short, projecting branch. *Rip!* Pete hit the ground safely, but his trousers were badly torn.

"Good night!" he exclaimed. "Now what'll I do?"

"I'll mend the tear right away," Mrs. Hollister offered.

"I have an idea," Jim said. "Pete, while your mother's sewing, suppose you come to my room and try on the outfit I wore in the New Year's parade."

"Okay. Let's go."

The three men excused themselves to return to Mr. Davis' office with the Soaring Satellite. The others went across the street. Pete and Jim hurried to the Chinese boy's room. Jim carried the torn trousers to Mrs. Hollister, who had returned home with the other children. Then Jim went back and showed Pete the holiday outfit. Pete slipped into it.

"This is nifty," Pete grinned, looking in a mirror. The satin costume consisted of red baggy pantaloons and collared Oriental jacket, buttoned high to the neck.

"Pretty fancy for a parade," Pete remarked.

Jim told him that various boys' clubs in Chinatown dressed in uniforms like this at the New Year celebration and followed the prancing dragons through the streets.

"Maybe Pam would like to try on a Chinese outfit," Jim said.

"I guess the others would, too," Pete replied.

Jim called them into his apartment. They laughed and clapped upon seeing Pete and were eager to be dressed as Chinese. The twins supplied them with costumes.

"I'm a Chinese at last!" Sue said. "Oh, I must get my coolie hat to go with this black and gold suit."

Sue skipped out of the Foos' apartment to show her mother the costume and get the hat. A moment later she raced back, wild-eyed and panting with excitement.

"Why, Sue, what's the matter? You look as if you've seen a dragon!" Pam said.

"C-come quick!" Sue cried out, her arms waving wildly. "Hong Yee is here!"

CHAPTER 17

AN IMPORTANT PUSH BUTTON

"Hong Yee in our apartment? I can't believe it," Pam declared.

"He is! Really, he is!" said Sue, reaching for her sister's hand. "Hurry!"

Wild thoughts raced through the minds of the youngsters. Was Hong Yee giving himself up and returning the missing note? Or had something terrible happened to Hootnanny Gandy?

When they burst into the Hollister apartment, Pete and Pam stopped short in utter amazement. The man standing in the living room talking to their mother was not the Hong Yee they had seen in Shoreham and again in Chinatown. But he looked very much like the person who had been thwarting the efforts of the Hollisters to solve the mystery.

"Children," Mrs. Hollister said, "I would like you to meet the real Mr. Hong Yee. He is from San Francisco."

Pete spoke up politely. "How do you do, sir?" then added, "What does Mother mean, 'the real Mr. Hong Yee'?"

"The man you know as Hong Yee is an impostor," the caller stated. "He's trying to take my place."

"Oh!" the Hollisters gasped.

Mr. Hong Yee shook hands and bowed slightly as he met each of the Hollister children. Then he spoke a few words in Chinese to Jim and Kathy.

"Mr. Yee has something very interesting to tell you," Mrs. Hollister declared.

The Chinese caller took a seat and the children sat cross-legged on the floor to listen. "First of all," he said, "the Hong Yee who has been bothering you is not Chinese at all."

"Kathy, Jim, you were right!" Pam exclaimed. She told Hong Yee of the Foos' astute observation of the impostor.

"Others besides you Hollisters have been fooled by the man's clever make-up," Hong Yee said. "His real name is Ralph Jones. I learned this through a company from which I import jade from Singapore. Jones was hiding in China for a while because the police in the United States wanted him. He picked up enough of the Chinese language to sound convincing. As your mother has told you, I live in San Francisco. When bank checks I had not written were being received for payment, I realized that someone was impersonating me and forging my name."

"What a dreadful thing to do!" Pam exclaimed.

"Yes," the Chinese agreed. "Your Shoreham police gave me the first clue to Ralph Jones. He told a clerk in a Shoreham store he was from San Francisco. But the clerk was suspicious later when he saw the man driving a car with New York license plates and reported this to the police."

"We'll put a stop to this when we catch him," Pete said. "Will you help us find him, Mr. Hong Yee?"

"Indeed, yes," the Chinese replied. "Ralph Jones

is a dangerous person. He stole some identification cards of mine. I didn't know this for some time. The sooner he is caught, the better."

As Mrs. Hollister went to the kitchen to prepare tea for their caller, Pete followed. He asked his mother if he might tell Mr. Hong Yee all the details of their mystery. Mrs. Hollister nodded, adding that she had examined the man's identification and felt him to be an honest person. "Besides, Officer Cal directed him to us."

Pete returned to the living room and said, "Maybe you will help us solve a mystery."

"I'll be happy to."

Step by step, Pete outlined what had happened to the Happy Hollisters from the moment they had purchased the book on New York tunnels at the sale in Shoreham. When the boy came to the part about the mysterious note concerning the statue of Kuan Yen, the Chinese said, "Ah, yes, Kuan Yen, the Goddess of Mercy." He added that some Orientals of several generations before had used the statues as secret hiding places.

Pete's heart thumped. Did the statue itself hold the treasure?

Hong Yee told the children that some statues of Kuan Yen had intricate carvings which often concealed a secret button. When pressed, the button started a mechanism that made some section of the statue spring out. Behind it was a secret hiding place.

"Please, come with us right away so we can try to find one," Pete urged.

"I'm sorry," Hong Yee said, rising. "I have an appointment with some jade merchants and I will not be able to look at the statue until tomorrow morning. But I will come, I promise." The man smiled. "I would like to find a treasure, but most of all I want to catch the impostor, Ralph Jones!"

Pete hoped that together they might achieve both goals and told him this.

"That is my sincere wish," Hong Yee said as he stepped out of the apartment. He smiled at the Foo twins. *"Ho-sai-kai."*

"Good luck to you, too, Mr. Hong Yee," Pam spoke up, smiling mischievously.

Mr. Yee looked pleased. "So you have learned some Chinese! Very good!"

The evening hours seemed to drag. Not once did the Hollisters forget the mystery. They worried about Hootnanny Gandy, and finally Pam telephoned the police department. She was told that no trace of the man had been found.

"We'll let you know if we have any word," the officer on duty said. But none came, and as the Hollisters went to bed that evening, they said a special prayer for the safety of the old tunnel digger.

True to his promise, Hong Yee appeared at the apartment next morning shortly after breakfast. The Foo twins were already there. Mr. Hollister was introduced and said, smiling, "Did you have a successful meeting with the jade merchants?"

"Yes, thank you," Hong Yee replied. "I hope my luck continues today."

"We do too," Pete spoke up. "Are you ready to go now, sir?"

At a nod from the Chinese, all the children filed out with him. Sue had begged to join the searchers, and her mother had said she might go. Gleefully she cried out, "We'd better hurry! We don't want the bad man to get there ahead of us!"

The same disturbing thought occurred to Pete as he hurried along Pell Street and entered Miss Helen's shop. Ralph Jones, the impostor, was clever. Suppose he had somehow managed to find the treasure already! Then all the Hollisters' sleuthing would have been in vain.

But to their relief the serene figure of the wooden goddess appeared undisturbed. Quickly Pam told Miss Helen the latest news. "This is the real Mr. Hong Yee," she said, introducing the two. "He thinks maybe there's a hiding place in the statue and a concealed button to open it."

"Ah, yes," Hong Yee said, as he approached the statue of Kuan Yen in the back of the gift shop. "It is a very fine specimen."

The shopkeeper looked on in amazement as Hong Yee's slender fingers flitted over the surface of the goddess' statue. Every little nook and cranny in the intricate scrollwork was probed by the Chinese. Finally, he said, "The secret button is well hidden. Will you children help me find it?"

Immediately, eager young hands began to examine the exquisite carving. Pete, being the tallest, searched the head carefully. Even little Sue did her part. Squat-

In stepped Hootnanny Gandy!

173

ting on the base, she ran her fingers over the feet of Kuan Yen. "Oh, dear," she sighed. "Poor Kuan Yen has a bump."

"A bump?" Pam cried out. "Where, Sue?"

"Right here on her little toe."

Pam bent down to examine the carving. On the right foot of the statue was a tiny welt, hardly larger than a mosquito bite. Pam pushed her thumb against it, hoping breathlessly that something would happen.

Suddenly, the searchers were electrified by a clicking, whirring sound. At the same time, Kuan Yen started to move forward away from the wall. Everyone watched, fascinated. In a moment the wooden goddess stopped moving.

Mr. Hong Yee was the first to speak. "Sue, you surely have bright eyes. And now we must find out what has been revealed."

To everyone's disappointment, the statue was intact and nothing was hidden between Kuan Yen and the wall.

"Yikes!" Ricky said. "There isn't any treasure!"

"Or tunnel either," Kathy remarked.

Pete, however, was not ready to give up, and set about to examine the wall. It was made of wood and showed no signs of indentations or secret openings to a tunnel.

"Now what!" Jim said, with a sigh. As he spoke, the front door opened.

In stepped Hootnanny Gandy!

"You're safe! I'm so glad!" Pam cried out, as they all rushed forward to meet him.

"Hi, kids!" he called cheerily.

"Hootnanny!" Pete exclaimed. "Where have you been? How did you get away?"

The old sand hog told them that he had found himself wandering on a street in Greenwich Village. The men who had taken him away had hidden him in a cellar overnight. They had tried to force him to tell about the secret tunnel.

"I didn't do it, though," Hootnanny said. "Couldn't remember worth a hootnanny. Then," he continued, "they hit me hard and I kind of got cobwebs in my brain for a while. But when the cobwebs cleared away, then I remembered!"

"The tunnel?" Pete asked hopefully.

"Yep. It's right here in front of your noses." He pointed to the blank wall behind Kuan Yen. The old fellow strode over and felt the wall with the palm of his hand. Far down in the right hand corner he pointed to a pair of letters, crudely whittled into the wood. They were H G.

"My trademark," Hootnanny said, grinning. "The tunnel's right behind this wall."

"Hooray! Hooray!" Ricky shouted.

"May we break it down, Miss Helen?" Pete asked the shopkeeper.

"Yes, yes, go ahead, do," she said. "Goodness, I've never been so excited in my life!"

Their faces flushed with excitement, Hong Yee and the boys began to tear strips of wood from the wall. If the treasure was inside, what was it? Pete could hardly wait. But suddenly he heard a sound which sent a chill through him.

"Listen!" he called out.

Hootnanny and the others stopped while Pete pressed his ear to the wall. From the other side came sounds, *Thump, thump, thump!*

"Somebody's digging in there!" Pete cried out.

"Ralph Jones!" Pam guessed.

"If it is," Pete said, "he's trying to reach the treasure ahead of us!"

CHAPTER 18

A FIRECRACKER TRICK

"Hurry!" cried Hootnanny Gandy. "We must get there first!"

The girls joined in helping to tear down the wooden wall. As they all worked, the old sand hog recalled that he had dug an opening at the other end of the tunnel. At Yuen Foo's request he had later filled this in. Whoever was burrowing into the passage from the other side must have learned about the former opening!

"Where was the exit?" Pam asked.

"In the back yard. An iron grating covers it."

"We must have somebody guard it," Pete said, "in case the digger tries to escape."

"I'll do it!" Hong Yee said. "I want to capture Ralph Jones!"

The jade merchant went out the back door while the others worked furiously. Finally the wall gave way, revealing a gaping black hole and a short tunnel.

"Where does this lead?" Jim asked Hootnanny.

"To a secret chamber, right ahead of us. Have you a flashlight, Miss Helen?"

"Yes." She handed one to Hootnanny and the old fellow beamed the light ahead. In its glare could be seen a bolted door. In the center was a sliding panel which Hootnanny pushed aside. The opening was hardly wide enough for a boy to get through. Pete looked through it into a small room.

The flashlight beam flitted over the back of a man. He was snatching an object from a table. Quickly he retreated through an opening on the other side of the secret chamber.

"Stop!" Pete demanded, but the intruder obviously had no intention of getting caught. "I'll go through," Pete said.

As Hootnanny handed him the light, Jim insisted he was going too. The two boys wriggled into the chamber. The tunnel on the opposite side loomed black and gloomy. But Pete could see where the shadowy intruder had recently dug through a dirt barrier to enter the room.

"Stop! Come back, whoever you are!" he called out.

As the boys progressed through the dark tunnel, they could hear Hootnanny breaking down the door behind them.

Suddenly Pete and Jim came to a fork in the tunnel. Which one to follow? The larger opening went to the left. The boys took it. Now, however, the passage grew smaller, and Pete had to stoop low to make his way through. At the end of it four bars of light showed through an overhead grate.

"Hong Yee!" Pete called up. "Did you catch him?"

"Nobody came out!"

"Oh, oh," Pete whispered. "That impostor must have taken the other fork in the tunnel by mistake."

Shivers went up the boys' spines as they wriggled around in the narrow passage to make their way back.

If the prowler was trapped, he might fight like a cornered animal—especially if he had the treasure!

Coming to the fork again, Pete and Jim saw the other branch of the tunnel gaping before them. They stopped and listened. Both were sure they could detect the sound of heavy breathing. This was obscured, however, by the muffled shouts of Hootnanny and the other children. They had broken down the small door and were now coming along the tunnel toward them.

"Pete! Jim! Where are you?" Hootnanny called.

"Right here, at the fork in the tunnel."

Hootnanny told Ricky and the girls to linger behind. He came forward and held a council of war with Pete and Jim.

"Do you remember digging this fork?" Pete asked the old sand hog.

"Yep, I do," came his answer. He told the boys that the small fork had been dug first, but a large boulder had barred the progress. Then Hootnanny had dug the other arm of the tunnel, which led to the yard.

"Jim and I don't think our man has escaped," Pete whispered. "We believe he's in the dead end tunnel."

"I guess we'd better get the police," Hootnanny suggested.

"I have a different idea," Pete whispered. "Maybe it'll work."

"What is it?" Jim asked.

Pete thrust his hand into a pocket and pulled out the packet of firecrackers which Jim had given him several days before. "We can blast him out with these."

"It's worth a try," Hootnanny said. He showed his light along the dank tunnel wall. The light stabbed through until it came to a bend. Pete thought the criminal might be hiding there.

Borrowing a match from Hootnanny, Pete lighted the fuse, then quickly threw the firecrackers down the length of the tunnel.

Bang-bang-bang-crack!

Instantly, the place was filled with shot-like reports. Bright yellow flashes illuminated the darkness. The noise was deafening; the light blinding.

Suddenly, a voice cried out from inside the tunnel, "I give up! I can't face a machine gun!"

"Come out with your hands up!" Hootnanny ordered.

A figure moved in the darkness, then the flashlight beam fell full on the face of Ralph Jones, the false Hong Yee. He was carrying a birdlike object in his hands.

As he came forward, Pete took the object from him. Hootnanny whipped off his belt and bound the captive's hands. At the shop end of the tunnel, the other children waited expectantly. They had heard the firecrackers, but had no idea what Pete had done.

When the group came out with their prisoner, Ricky shouted, "You caught him!"

"He's the mean man!" Holly said.

Miss Helen instantly went to the phone to call the police. Meanwhile, Pete placed the heavy birdlike

Ricky shouted, "You caught him!"

object on the counter. Pam found a cloth and wiped the dirt from it.

Hong Yee hurried in and berated the prisoner for impersonating him. When the merchant's eyes fell on the figure, he grasped it and cried out, "A hawk! A jade hawk! This is a fabulous treasure!"

"So that's the 'great bird' old Yuen Foo was hiding from his enemies," Pam said.

Hong Yee estimated its value in thousands of dollars. "Whoever owns the jade hawk possesses a fortune indeed," he told the wide-eyed group.

Miss Helen stepped forward instantly. To Kathy and Jim she said, "And the owner of this precious bird is your father, Paul Foo. Kuan Yen has guarded it well for your family."

The Foo twins exchanged looks of joy, then turned to the Hollisters. "Our friends," Kathy said, smiling at them. "How can we ever thank you for bringing us such good fortune?"

"We're happy we could help," Pam replied modestly.

But how did Ralph Jones know of Yuen Foo's secret, everyone wondered.

The prisoner now looked less like a Chinese than he ever had before. Black eyebrow pencil was smeared on his forehead and putty cheekbones stuck askew from his face.

By this time Officer Hobbs had rushed into the shop. He was amazed to hear the story. When the prisoner heard about the firecrackers, he thrashed around angrily until the officer's strong grip subdued him. "To think a kid captured me with firecrackers!" he moaned.

"I'd say it was very good strategy," the patrolman added with a grin. "And now, Jones, suppose you tell us the name of your pal and what this is all about. If you confess, things will go easier for you and your friend."

Thoroughly dejected and frightened, Ralph Jones spoke freely, "I want to get it off my chest. I'll tell you everything."

Ten years before, he said, when he lived in China, he had made friends with Yuen Foo. The old man was very sick and gave Jones all the money he had to take care of him. "It was a lot," Jones went on. "Just before Foo died, he asked me to mail a letter to his son Paul for him but instead I opened it. The letter contained the message instructing Paul to look in the old book on tunnels for a secret note."

"When I found out there was a treasure, I decided to get it for myself and not send the letter. The police nearly caught me robbing a store, so I had to hide a while. I didn't get to this country for several years.

"Finally I shipped into San Francisco, broke. That's when I took some identification cards of Hong Yee's. I'd seen him in Singapore and thought it would be easy to impersonate him. I managed to cash some checks using his name. That's how I had enough money to get to New York and buy a car. Got the license, too, with Hong Yee's name."

"Your make-up didn't fool Kathy and Jim," Holly spoke up proudly. "They knew you aren't Chinese."

Jones continued with his story, telling how he had traced the book. He had sent a pal to try buying it from Paul Foo and learned that he had lent it to a friend named Smith. This man in turn had lost the book without discovering the note. Smith must have forgotten leaving the volume in the Chens' restaurant.

Pam asked the prisoner, "How did you find out the book on tunnels was in Shoreham?"

Jones actually smiled. "Pretty smart of me, eh?" he asked. "Smith was a traveling salesman. Recently I followed him from town to town to see where he usually stopped. I asked in the various places if he had left the book. Finally I located it in Shoreham."

A glum expression once more came over the prisoner's face. "If you Hollisters hadn't bought that book, I might have had this treasure for myself."

Jones said he had learned the Hollisters were good detectives and intended to come to Chinatown. He had eavesdropped on them in Shoreham and had his pal follow Pete and Ricky in the taxi. "I tried to stop you kids from searching," he said, "but it didn't work."

Jim looked proudly at his new friends. "It takes more than that to stop the Hollisters!" he said.

"Who took Hootnanny away in the cab?" Pam asked.

Jones hung his head, and admitted that he and his pal, "Spike" Conlon, had snatched Hootnanny. "We let him go when we found the secret," Jones said.

"I gave you the secret?" Hootnanny asked in surprise.

The prisoner declared that after they had struck the old man, Hootnanny became semi-conscious. He had babbled the story of the grating in the garden and said that without too much trouble a breakthrough could be made.

"So that's how you got into the secret chamber!" Jim said.

Pete also had a question. "Where did you disappear the time we chased you through the hallway?"

Jones answered, "I wasn't always a thief. I once was an acrobat in a circus."

"Pam, you guessed right!" Kathy said. "That's how he got up the fire escape and over the rooftops."

While this conversation had been going on, Officer Hobbs had phoned for a police van. Now two officers arrived and took Jones away.

Jim now told Miss Helen he knew that his father would replace the damaged wall in the store. "Unless you want to keep the tunnel," he said, grinning.

"No indeed," she said. "And I hope your father will take Kuan Yen. Now that I know the whole story, I hardly feel it belongs to me. It belongs to the Foo family as a great keepsake."

"That reminds me!" Pete exclaimed. "I was going to get another vase for the Chens." He looked about the shop and spotted an attractive Ming piece similar to the broken one. But it was very expensive. Pete's face fell. He would not be able to buy it.

Meanwhile, news of the great discovery spread quickly through Chinatown. Many residents of the area stopped by to congratulate the Hollisters.

Again and again the Foos thanked them for their excellent detective work. Mr. Foo sold the jade hawk to Hong Yee for a large sum.

"Now," said the twins' father, when he came to the Hollisters' apartment, "my children can be assured of going to college."

Then Kathy and Jim, who carried a large package, smiled at Pete. "Here's something for you to take back to Shoreham," said Jim.

Pete opened the package. "Crickets! The vase I wanted for the Chens!"

"Yes," Kathy said. "We heard how you broke the first one working on our mystery."

In the midst of the excitement, the doorbell rang. Mr. Hollister opened it to greet Mr. Davis.

"Hello, Charlie," he said. "Come in and listen to the good news."

When the story was told, Mr. Davis grinned. "Great!" he said. "And John, I have some good news for you too."

"What is it?"

"Our Soaring Satellite has out-orbited everything at the Coliseum Hobby Show. Come on, all of you. I'll take you up to see it."

Half an hour later the Hollisters and the Foos walked through the massive doors of a huge building at Broadway and Fifty-ninth Street.

"This is the Coliseum," Mr. Davis told them.

"The great exhibitions of New York are shown here."

The Hollisters had never seen anything like this before. After passing through a wide lobby, they stepped into a huge hall. Instead of being one story tall, it was two.

The place was filled with hobby exhibits of all kinds, and people thronged about. Most of them were gazing upward. Pete followed their glances.

"Hey, look!" he cried out. Near the ceiling drifted the toy moon, and about it circled the Soaring Satellite. Up it went and down it came as visitors manipulated the great new toy.

"And now another surprise," Charlie Davis beamed, as he put an arm about Mr. Foo's shoulder. "The Soaring Satellite, thanks to our Chinese friend here, has won the top prize in the Hobby Show."

Hearing this, all the children congratulated the men. Then Pam and Kathy flung their arms about each other. Grinning, Pete and Jim slapped each other on the shoulder. Holly and Sue clapped vigorously, while Ricky, about to cup his hands and yell out in his excitement, caught a look from his mother and stopped. Instead he went to shake hands with the men.

Suddenly Holly remarked, "I'm glad there aren't any windows in this place."

"Why?" Pam asked.

"Because I wouldn't want the Soaring Satellite to escape again."

Hearing this, everyone chuckled. Just at that moment the loudspeaker blared, and the voice said, "Will Mr. Davis, Mr. Hollister, and Mr. Foo please come forward to get their prize as collaborators in creating the world's newest toy, the Soaring Satellite?"

As the three men went forward to receive their award, Sue exclaimed in a loud, high voice, "I just love Skyscraper City!"

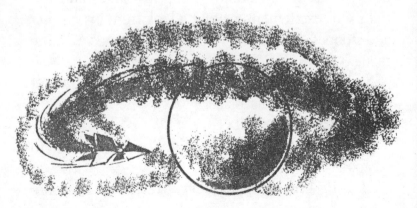